MERRY CHRISTMAS, DARLING

DONNA ALWARD

Merry Christmas, Darling
By Donna Alward

© Donna Alward 2019

1

If there was one thing the town of Darling, Vermont, knew how to do, it was Christmas. Wreaths and bows hung from the streetlamps. Storefronts were decorated with sparkly lights and holiday-themed wares, beckoning passersby to come inside. A Christmas tree sat on the Green beside Fisher Creek and next to the Kissing Bridge, waiting for the tree-lighting ceremony that would happen on the weekend. The air smelled like evergreen and cinnamon and butter cookies. There'd even been flurries overnight, covering the ground with a dusting of pristine snow. Everything looked like a greeting card, and normally, Hannah Gallagher loved every moment of it.

Instead, she let out a frustrated breath, hung up the phone, and slumped against the desk in her office.

The second annual literacy benefit was only three weeks away, and her celebrity author and speaker had just cancelled their appearance. The whole event had been planned around Jillian Jordan's attendance. And now…nothing.

Sure, having surgery was a legitimate excuse. She guessed. But it put her in a horrible pickle. Tickets for the event had already gone on sale. Donations for the silent auction were coming in, with others promised. Local businesses were in on the action. The literacy benefit was her brainchild, her baby, and last year had been a roaring success, raising thousands for local literacy organizations. There was no way she wanted the event to suffer a sophomore slump.

She had to find another celebrity. Someone who didn't mind traveling to a small town in Vermont in three weeks, and a week before Christmas to boot. Someone willing to donate their time, who wasn't already booked up. And someone who would be the *right* person, not just anyone who could fill a chair or stand up to the mic. She'd originally begun this process in March. Now she had to do it all again in a matter of days.

"I hate my life, I hate my life, I hate my life," she muttered, resting her forehead on the heel of her hand.

"Aw, it can't be all bad."

Hannah lifted her head and found Oaklee Collier standing in her doorway, her blond hair pulled into a perfect topknot, one hip resting on the doorframe, and a lopsided smile on her otherwise symmetrical face.

If Hannah had anything to say about it, Oaklee would be her sister-in-law one of these days. She heartily approved of her brother Rory's choice in partners.

"Jillian Jordan just cancelled. She's having surgery in ten days and doesn't think she'll be recovered enough to attend the benefit."

Oaklee's smile disappeared from her face. "Oh, shit."

"Shit is right. Can you think of a replacement? And I don't want it to be us scraping the bottom of the barrel for anyone with a pulse, you know?"

"Of course." Oaklee came farther into the office and sat in the chair opposite Hannah's desk. "I mean, do we have to have a celebrity?"

"Yes?" Hannah pursed her lips. "I'm just…not angry. I can't be angry with a woman who has to have medical treatment, can I? But *why*?" She drew out the last word and punctuated it with a sigh.

Oaklee leaned forward. "You'll figure it out, Han. You always do. No one gets stuff done like you do. You're General Gallagher. You just need to round up your troops."

Hannah stared at Oaklee. General Gallagher? She'd been called a lot of things over the years, and for some reason, this one bothered her a lot. Yes, she was definitely type A. She didn't feel she should apologize for it. She had skills. But the two monikers she'd earned that she disliked the most was this one and Dozer. As in bulldozer. Which was just slightly worse, in her view, than Ballbuster.

She was a doer. She got things done. And that way, she didn't have to focus too much on her non-existent love life. Because in that one area, she was an absolute failure. She had the battle scars to prove it. Hell, an ex was where the Dozer name came from.

"If you start calling me General, I'll fire you."

"You can't fire me. I'm a volunteer."

Hannah angled an eyebrow in Oaklee's direction. "You know what I mean."

Oaklee sat back and studied Hannah, intensely enough that Hannah started to be a bit uncomfortable. "What?"

"It really bothered you, didn't it? I'm sorry. I was just teasing."

Hannah let out a breath. "I know. Don't worry about it. I'm just touchy. I really didn't need this today."

Oaklee leaned forward and reached out to touch Hannah's arm. "I know, sweetie. Listen, I popped in to ask you if you wanted to grab a drink at Suds and Spuds later. Do you want to? Maybe we can brainstorm then."

Hannah nodded. Oaklee was an invaluable volunteer. She managed the town's social media and worked with their marketing and promotions department. She also knew how to get results and be part of a team. She'd designed the event website and Facebook page, and then all the promotional materials…

Ugh. Another thought darted into Hannah's brain. All the signage would have to be redone. Considering the print costs had been donated, it put another layer of wrinkles into the situation. Maybe she could find another sponsor.

"A beer sounds perfect." She wouldn't worry about the calories until tomorrow. "I have a showing at six thirty. Say seven thirty-ish?"

Oaklee got up from her chair and smoothed her hand down her sweater. "That sounds perfect. Rory works late tonight anyway. I just have to run home and feed the dog after work."

Oaklee and Rory had been living together for close to six months. Hannah's younger brother was a veterinarian. He'd given up his bachelor digs above the clinic and bought a house two blocks away from their brother, Ethan, and his family. Oaklee had moved in with him over the summer when the lease on her townhouse was up. They had a dog and a variety of cats or other animals that Rory usually ended up bringing home from the clinic from time to time.

Everyone was settling down. Or at least all the boys in the family were. Hannah was the oldest female and completely single. Her twin sisters, in their early twenties, weren't interested in settling down yet. Heck, Cait hadn't ever had a boyfriend. She was more interested in hanging out with friends than relationships.

But at thirty-three, Hannah was starting to hear a ticking clock and resigning herself to being Fun Aunt Hannah for her nieces and nephews. Certainly no one in Darling was willing to take her on. And there was no one she was interested in, either.

"Perfect. I'll see you then. I'm glad you stopped by, Oaklee. I'm not quite as panicked as I was when I hung up that phone."

"You'll figure it out. You always do. I'll catch you later."

She left with a waggle of her fingers, leaving Hannah in her quiet office. It was too quiet. The real estate market was a bit slow right now, and her office assistant had gone home at noon since her daughter got sick at school. A few doors down, The Purple Pig Café did a bustling business of coffee, hot chocolate, and gingerbread lattes for the Christmas season, replacing the pumpkin spice flavor from Thanksgiving. She considered going for a tea and a scone and then decided against. She could make tea right here and work until she had to leave for her showing. Besides, she was feeling rather cranky and was inclined to stay in her office rather than have to be out in public with her outward facing, energetic, and positive persona.

Sometimes it got tiring being Hannah Gallagher.

She put on the kettle and plopped a peppermint tea bag in a mug, then grabbed a handful of grapes from the fridge and sat back in her chair, the casters making a slight squeak as she pulled it closer to the desk.

With a click of her mouse, she opened up her browser and started a search. Finding a replacement wouldn't happen all on its own. If she was going to be lonely, at least she could be productive doing it.

CAM COLLIER HAD BEEN HOME EXACTLY TWICE IN THE last five years. And each time, he was surprised to find that nothing had really changed in Darling. Cute town, friendly people, same stores and shops. Slow, too. He was used to being in Denver, a bigger city with a lot more going on. Heck, Darling didn't even have a movie theater.

He turned off Main Street with its decorated street-lamps and storefronts and went across a bridge, then over to the other end of the park. One thing Darling did have, however, was an ice rink. It had been as much a home to him as anywhere in town, and that included his own house and that of the Gallaghers. As a kid, if anyone wanted to find Cam, it was in one of those three places.

Rory Gallagher had been his best friend for years, until Cam had moved away in high school to play major junior hockey. After that, he'd been drafted to St. Louis as a second-round pick. Traded to Boston. And for the last few years, he'd been in Denver, wearing the big C on his chest. He'd had a fairy-tale career, really. Some playoff runs and a Stanley Cup. One of his two trips home had been after that win, when he got to bring the cup for a visit. It had been surreal for a guy of twenty-six. There'd been a parade.

He'd also taken a few rough hits. He'd been side-lined for knee and shoulder injuries, though they'd been minor, and he'd been back on the ice quickly. This time was different. This was concussion number two, thanks to a cross-check that had nailed him into the boards. They were only eight weeks into the regular season, and he was now benched until cleared by the doctors.

At twenty-nine, he still had a lot of career left. Another head injury after this one, and he could be side-lined permanently.

The rink was quiet now, the parking lot empty with the exception of Cam's rented SUV. Weekdays weren't busy. All the kids were in school. Oh, there was ice time in the morning, and after school, and in the evenings there'd be practice, since the high school team used the rink as their home ice as well. And on the weekends, the lot would be crammed. But right now, it was quiet. Cam shut the car door and walked to the entrance, his feet crunching on the light dusting of snow that had come this week, just a few days after Thanksgiving.

The door was open, and Cam figured there was a custodian on duty or something. He made his way to the middle of the seats—all benches—and stopped where he could look over center ice.

It had all started here. Skating lessons at age three. A hockey stick in his hand at age four. Hockey had been in his blood from the beginning. In some ways, it was all he'd ever known. The one thing he could count on.

And now he was home, feeling uncertain and already missing his team. Missing the ice under his blades and the feel of the stick in his gloved hands. The sound of skates cutting up the ice; the smooth sheen of it after the Zamboni did its work.

He was home because the doctors had told him that he absolutely needed to take time to recuperate or else there would be no more hockey. And a world without hockey was…inconceivable.

His sister, Oaklee, had convinced him to come home for Christmas. She and Rory were hosting a New Year's Eve party, and there wasn't a hope that he'd be cleared for play that soon. He'd been put on four weeks of medical leave. After that, he'd only be cleared for practice if he stayed symptom free. Once everyone was confident in his ability to return, he'd be put back in the lineup.

Four weeks in Darling.

He wasn't sure he was going to make it. But his folks were thrilled he was going to be home for the holidays. He was at least glad he could make them happy about that. And he'd be eating his mom's cooking, too. Her spaghetti and meatballs and the Christmas shortbread she made each year.

But not playing hockey.

Some people got holiday depression. Cam didn't. But this year, he had anxiety, and it had little to do with Christmas. He was worried his fear of another injury would cause him to lose his edge. He had two more years left on his contract. If it wasn't renewed, he'd be a free agent. Or he'd have to consider…retirement. But the check still loomed in his mind. The sight of the other player in the corner of his eye. The force of the impact, and then…nothing. He didn't remember blacking out, or regaining consciousness, or leaving the ice on a stretcher because of the possibility of a neck injury. Instead, he'd seen the news replays. Every time, he got a horrible sick feeling in the pit of his stomach.

But if he wanted to play, he couldn't play afraid.

He took a big breath and let it out slowly, trying to push the thoughts away. Right now, he was at the rink, breathing in the cool air, remembering sweet memories from his childhood. He was here, and he might as well make the best of it. If recovering was what he had to do, he'd do the best job of it ever.

Because failure was absolutely not on the agenda.

When he had restored himself with the cool sounds and scents of the rink, he returned to his SUV and made the five-minute drive to his parents' place. The house was small by most standards, barely over a thousand square feet of bungalow, with three bedrooms, a single bathroom, and an oversized deck overlooking the back yard. He kept offering to buy or build them a new house, something that wasn't built in the eighties and with more amenities. But they insisted they liked it just fine, so here they stayed.

He got out of the SUV and stood for a moment, breathing in the crisp, cool air. Thank God, he'd been cleared to drive. It was bad enough he couldn't play. That his life was on hold. At least he had some freedom.

But for now, he was home for the holidays, and moping about it wasn't doing his mood any favors. Maybe he needed to start counting his blessings instead. Including time spent with his parents and sister.

"Cam? Is that you?"

A smile broke out on his face at the excited sound of his mother's voice, and his heart lightened. "Yeah, Mom, it's me." He rounded the hood and went up the short drive, his shoes leaving footprints in the dusting of snow on the paved surface. His mom wore a huge grin and opened her arms to him.

"About time you came home for Christmas."

"I know, I know." He enfolded her smaller body in a big hug and then set her back, holding her by the arms. "You look good, lady." She was graying a little bit, and her laugh lines were getting a little deeper, but she looked happy and healthy.

She laughed. "Go on." Then her laugh softened, and she peered up at him. "Be honest. How're you feeling?"

He shrugged, deciding he might as well tell her everything. She'd get it out of him anyway. "Tired. Frustrated I can't play or even practice." He sighed. "Afraid of what lies ahead."

"You're not done playing yet. You just can't rush things. And you always like to rush things."

"I know." He smiled. "Let me get my stuff and come in. We can order something for dinner and hang out."

"Order?" She shook her head. "Don't even think about it. I made a roast for tonight. And cake."

He went back down the drive to the SUV and opened the tailgate. "What? You cooked?"

"Brat. I do know how, you know. I did it lots when I wasn't running to the rink all the time."

He knew it, but he loved bugging her about it anyway. "You mean I won't be eating frozen lasagna and Shepherd's Pie from a box?"

"If you didn't have a concussion, I'd box your ears."

He laughed again, and it felt good. Okay, so maybe this wasn't the best situation. But he did love his family, and it had been too long since he had a good visit.

His dad had retired, and Cam found him inside, watching the news channel. "Hey, Dad," he said, putting down his duffel and toeing off his shoes.

"Hey, yourself!" His dad rose and came to the entry. "Gosh, it's good to see you. How're you feeling?"

Cam figured he was going to get that question a lot,

so he might as well practice patience. "I'm okay. Feel fine, mostly. But restless."

"You're not used to sitting still. Even in the off-season, you're training. Gotta be tough."

Cam wasn't sure what he was going to do with himself for four weeks. Christmas shopping would take up an afternoon. There were doctor appointments already set up. But how would he fill his days?

His mom popped back in the foyer. "Your old room is ready for you, Cam."

Lord. He hadn't actually lived in this house for over a decade. He hefted his duffel and started down the hall, stopping in front of Oaklee's old room. He was looking forward to spending more time with her, actually. And Rory. They'd been together just over a year now, and once he'd got over the surprise of them hooking up, he could see how perfect they were for each other.

He wasn't jealous. Nope. Besides, he was traveling a lot, and trades meant moving cities. Lots of his team-mates were married with families, but he'd always thought a stable upbringing was better for kids.

Like he'd had.

His mom opened his bedroom door and he went inside, then turned around and hugged her again. "Thanks, Mom," he said.

She laughed. "For what?"

"For everything."

She stood back, and he thought he saw a glimmer of moisture in her eyes, but then she grinned. "That must have been some knock to the head," she quipped, winking at him. "You're all sentimental."

He smiled back but shook his head. "Naw, just realizing how much you guys sacrificed for me."

"Well, you're home for Christmas. Even if the reason isn't the best one, I'm glad to have you around for a while. Now you chill out, and I'll see you at dinner. You don't need me all up in your business."

He chuckled and nodded. She left and shut the door behind her, while he stood and surveyed his room—the double bed, plain chest of drawers, and a bookcase that held trophies rather than books.

Suddenly weary, he lay down on the bed and stared at the ceiling.

He was going to be bored out of his mind.

2

Hannah waited at the bar for a good fifteen minutes past their agreed time before Oaklee showed up. She'd sipped on water, but she was starving since she hadn't yet had dinner. She was dying for a plate of chili cheese fries. And then tomorrow she would do a longer run to work them off. Ninety-five percent of the time, she ate clean and said no to sugar and fried food. Tonight, though, she had zero willpower. The showing hadn't gone as well as she'd hoped, either. It had been a shit day all around.

Oaklee blew in on a cold breeze and peeled off her coat on the way to the table. "I'm sorry I'm late! I totally forgot I had a family dinner, and I thought I'd be finished on time. But Cam got telling stories, and I lost track of time."

"Cam's home?" Hannah lifted an eyebrow. Cam had always been Darling's golden boy. While he and Rory were best friends, Hannah could remember Cam being a bit big for his britches in school. She wondered if his ego was still as huge, considering what a superstar he was now.

"Yeah. He's off for a while. Another concussion." Oaklee's happy expression faded as she hung her coat over her chair. "He put on a good show, but I can tell he's worried."

"For how long?"

Oaklee sat and let out a breath. "Oh, well, he's home for the holidays. Going back to Denver after our New Year's party. You are coming to that, right?"

Hannah smiled. "Of course." She loved that Oaklee was already planning something a month away. She did the same thing. They really did get along well.

They each ordered a beer and Hannah ordered her fries, then the door opened again, and her sisters-in-law, Willow and Laurel, blew in. Hannah waved them over. "What are you guys doing here?"

Laurel shook a bit of snow off her hair. "We called Rory, and he said you guys were meeting here. The guys are watching the babies."

Willow had married Hannah's oldest brother, Ethan, and Laurel and Aiden had hooked up just before that and had a surprise wedding at the town's fabled Kissing Bridge. Hannah had always felt rather lucky that her best friends were now her sisters.

Food arrived, and another round of drinks, and before long, Hannah found herself relating her bad news about the benefit. "So we're without any sort of celebrity headliner, and only a few weeks to find a replacement."

Laurel tapped her fingernails on the table. "Hey, you

said Cam is home, right, Oaklee? Why not him? The kids around here would adore having him take part. He's like a local hero."

Hannah had been scouring her brain for a guest author, but the idea of having a famous athlete held appeal. Kids looked up to athletes as superstars. Having someone like Cam endorse reading? It would be a great thing.

"What do you think, Oaklee? Would he do it?"

"We can always ask. It wouldn't hurt. And it would solve your problem."

A weight seemed to lift off Hannah's shoulders. "I'll think about it. We could maybe have him do the reading at the library, you know? And then speak at the dinner. Maybe even donate a jersey or something to the auction."

Her day was starting to turn around. And all because Cam Collier had graced Darling with his presence for a few weeks. She'd never once considered Cam the kind of guy who would come to her rescue. But then she'd never in her life actually needed rescuing.

Right now, Cam could be the solution to all her problems.

HANNAH HADN'T QUITE DECIDED HOW TO BROACH THE topic with Cam, though she'd thought about it all through her morning run. She ran the same route every morning. She left her renovated colonial and headed toward downtown, then to the golf course, back up through the park, over the Kissing Bridge, down the Green to the Ladybug Garden Center, and then back along the main route into town. It was about four miles altogether, and Hannah considered the rhythmic sound of her breathing and the slap of her steps conducive to deep thinking. She solved a lot of problems during her run, but today, she'd conjured and dismissed a half dozen scenarios. She knew Cam, but they weren't exactly friends. She thought about getting Oaklee to facilitate some sort of meeting, where she could accidentally show up, but he'd see that ambush for what it was the moment she asked for the favor. Ditto with getting Rory involved as a middleman. She thought about showing up on the Colliers' doorstep and simply asking him, but she figured he got requests all the time and didn't want him to think she was cashing in on his celebrity—which of course, she was. Or wanted to, anyway.

No idea felt right, so she went home, showered, and left for work bundled in her warm coat, scarf, and her favorite knee-high boots. The cold weather was sticking around, and she didn't want to be frozen after her walk to the office.

Within minutes, she was inside the homey warmth of The Purple Pig Café for her daily coffee, with the scent of cinnamon and coffee around her. The display case showed a variety of muffins for the morning crowd, and she looked longingly at the blueberry-oat ones before ordering her coffee and, as her stomach growled, an egg-white breakfast sandwich and bowl of fruit salad.

Willow came out of the kitchen and lit up when she saw Hannah there.

"Morning, sunshine," her sister-in-law called, and moved to pour Hannah's coffee herself. "Long time no see."

Willow had opened The Purple Pig a few years ago, serving light, healthy fare that was organic and locally sourced. The menu was simple but satisfying, and the business had taken off. Then, when Willow and Ethan had their baby, she'd leased the space next door and opened a yoga studio. Nowadays, the running of the café largely fell to the manager, Emily. Seeing Willow behind the counter was a treat.

"Not teaching classes today, Wil?" Hannah took the coffee cup and sipped while she waited for her sandwich.

"I have a chair yoga class at the senior center at ten thirty," Willow said with a smile. "I stopped in to give Em a hand with the morning rush."

"And where's Brenna?" Willow and Ethan's daughter was just six months old and as cute as a bug's ear with Ethan's rusty hair and Willow's calm temperament.

"In her playpen in the back. I'll pop her to the sitter before my class." Willow tucked Hannah's sandwich in a paper bag, as well as the fruit salad and a spoon. "Here you go."

"Thanks," she said, just as a strange quiet settled over the busy café.

She turned around and immediately saw the reason

why. Cam had walked in the door, leaving the patrons gaping with expressions of what Hannah could say for certain was hero worship. And no wonder. She'd seen him on TV, of course, most often dressed in his hockey uniform and sweaty from playing. Not today. Today he was dressed in jeans and a bomber jacket that made his shoulders look impossibly wide. Hannah was tall at five-nine; Cam was well over six feet and made her feel small in comparison. It wasn't just his height or the way his ass looked in his jeans, though. He had ridiculously thick hair that curled just that little bit over the collar, and full lips that often smiled when he spoke on camera. Right now, they were smiling at the girl behind the counter, who was blushing to the roots of her hair as she took his order.

"That's him, isn't it?" Willow whispered close to Hannah's ear.

Hannah swallowed, her tongue suddenly thick and her throat dry. "Yeah," she managed, and felt ridiculous standing there gaping like some puck bunny. It had nothing to do with his fame, she realized, and everything to do with a simple visceral reaction to an incredibly sexy guy.

A guy who'd been four years behind her in school, and more of a cocky pain in her neck in those days than someone she'd like to—

"Hey, Hannah."

She stared up at him and felt uncharacteristic heat creep up her neck. "Oh, hey, Cam. I heard you were back in town."

Willow met Hannah's gaze and nodded, a knowing smile touching her lips. "Coffee, Cam?" She stuck out her hand. "I'm Willow, Ethan's partner."

He shook her hand and smiled easily. "I'd love some coffee to go with my breakfast."

"You got it."

Hannah was so relieved by Willow's rescue. It gave her a chance to get her head on straight and stop acting like a silly girl with a crush on the cute boy in chemistry class.

This was her opportunity to talk to Cam. She had to get her act together and be normal.

"Eating on the go?" Cam asked, making polite conversation. The crowd was talking again, but in a low hum, and watching Cam's every move. It would be comical if it weren't so disconcerting.

"I was going to take it back to my office, yeah." She smiled up at him. Lordy, she loved tall men. Always had.

"Oh. I was going to ask if you wanted to eat with me, but that's cool."

Hannah tried not to gawp and recovered as gracefully as she could as opportunity was dropped neatly into her lap. "Oh, well, sure."

He leaned forward. "If I sit alone, I'm going to feel like a spider under glass. Everyone staring and finding me incredibly fascinating and scary."

She snorted. "You? Scary?"

He gave a half shrug, and she couldn't help it, she was charmed. The way the crowd was acting right now, he might be right. He'd take his seat and go to eat, and everyone would stare.

A smile flirted with her lips. "I suppose I could take a few minutes for a bite."

"Go find a seat," Willow instructed. "I'll bring your food out when it's up, Cam."

"Thanks." He sent her a wide smile and then let Hannah lead the way to a small table toward the back of the small dining area.

She made her way to the table, her stomach in strange little knots. Odd. Nervousness was not generally her thing. Then again, this could be the serendipitous opportunity she'd been waiting for, couldn't it? And if that were the case, the success of the benefit relied on how well this meeting went. It had absolutely nothing to do with Cam Collier and his big shoulders and crazy sexy hair.

They were just at the table when Cam spoke up. "So is your office nearby?"

"Actually, it's just a few steps away." She gestured with her hand, forgot she was holding the coffee, and a bit sloshed over the rim and onto her hand.

It was *really* hot.

But she wouldn't let on. Instead, she reached for a chair with her free hand and put the coffee on the table, surreptitiously wiping her wet hand on her coat.

Great start, Hannah.

She put down her bag and shrugged out of her coat, hanging it over the back of the chair. She was really glad she'd worn her favorite sweater dress today. It was a knit column that hugged her figure and was in a soft gray that went extraordinarily well with her fiery hair. When she went to sit down, she caught Cam's gaze. It was warm and approving, and there was a snap of chemistry between them she couldn't—and didn't want to—deny. That they found each other visually appealing was quite nice, really. So what if she was older than him? There came an age when that didn't matter anymore, right?

"You look good, Hannah," he said quietly, his voice a low rumble so no one nearby could hear.

The fizz from a moment ago turned into spark that sizzled along her limbs and settled in her core.

"So do you, Cam." She lifted an eyebrow and gave him a sideways smile. "Really good."

"It's the five a.m. workouts," he replied, taking a sip of his coffee. "Never thought I'd say this, but I miss them."

She tried not to think about him in a gym. To be honest, his physicality was a huge turn on. Not that she was ever going to act on this. He was Rory's best friend, for heaven's sake. And even cancelling out the age difference, there was the sheer fact that Hannah didn't do flings. Didn't do relationships at all, really. Besides, after Christmas, Cam was headed straight back to Denver to finish out the season.

She wanted him for the benefit. Nothing more.

They'd only been seated for a few minutes when Willow brought out Cam's eggs and turkey sausage. Hannah now wished she'd got something other than a breakfast sandwich. She could just imagine lifting it to take a bite and having cheese stick to her mouth or something drip into her lap. She removed it from the bag and opened the wrapper, gathering the English muffin into her hands and hoping for the best.

She had just taken a nibble when a small voice sounded at her elbow. "'Scuse me, but can I have your autograph?"

The little guy couldn't have been more than seven, cute as anything, with a cowlick, a missing middle tooth, and sparkly blue eyes.

"Sure," Cam answered easily. "I don't have paper. Is a napkin okay?"

The little head bobbed so fast Hannah was surprised he didn't get whiplash.

"Do you play hockey?" Cam asked, while Hannah handed him a pen, a goofy smile on her lips.

"Uh huh. I started last year."

"Cool. You play at the rink here?"

Another enthusiastic nod.

Cam signed the napkin and held it out. "I learned to play hockey here, too. Here you go."

"Thanks!" The kid looked at Cam as if he hung the moon and the stars and then dashed away. Hannah heard him exclaim to his parents, "He signed a napkin! Cool!"

"Does that happen a lot?" she asked.

He laughed. "Yeah. But it's cool. I was that age once."

"It's good to be home, then?"

He regarded her with a strange expression. "Well, I guess. Except for the concussion and all."

Heat crept up her neck. What was wrong with her? What a dumb question. "Of course." She smiled and covered her embarrassment as smoothly as she could.

"Not the best circumstances for you at all. But still, your family must be glad to see you. And Rory, too."

He lifted his coffee cup and looked toward the window. "Sure. There's nothing like a Darling Christmas."

There was something in his voice that didn't quite ring true, and it left an awkward hole in the conversation.

Cam eventually filled the gap. "So Oaklee says you run the real estate office here in town."

"Just a few doors away." She was also a silent partner in Willow's yoga studio. Hannah wasn't the kind to shy away from opportunities.

"You always were independent and driven." He speared a piece of egg with his fork. "I'm not surprised you're running your own business rather than working for some corporation somewhere. You always struck me as someone who would like being their own boss."

She put down her sandwich and picked up her coffee. "Huh. I never thought you would have noticed. I mean, I was graduating high school when you were a freshman. And then you left town."

He met her gaze, and the lopsided grin returned. "Hannah. I was a fourteen-year-old boy whose best friend had a smokin' hot older sister. I noticed."

The blush from earlier came rushing back up her neck and face again. "Oh. Well."

He laughed and cut into a sausage link. "You didn't expect me to be so honest."

"Not really." Hannah was normally so calm and

collected, but in Cam's presence, she seemed to lose her self-assurance. Besides, it wasn't as if she could say the same. He'd always been cute, but he'd been her little brother's best friend. At eighteen, she hadn't exactly been interested in boys. She'd wanted to be an adult, go to university and date *men*. Not kids who were just learning to shave.

Eighteen to fourteen was a huge age gap. Thirty-three to twenty-nine was not the same. Especially when the man across the table was confident, successful, and at the top of his game.

His gaze held hers for a long moment, until Hannah found it hard to take a full breath. When she could hardly stand it anymore, she dropped her eyes to her sandwich and picked it up in her hands, uncharacteristically self-conscious.

"Relax," he said, his voice low. "It was just a compliment."

Was it? She wasn't so sure. Maybe if she actually dated, she'd navigate this kind of conversation better. Was he flirting? Or was it simply conversation? She could handle land deals with no problem. Coordinate special events and run a chamber of commerce meeting in her sleep. But flirting, sexual undertones, and subtext? She sucked at it. Probably because, according to her ex, she was a ballbuster, and guys didn't want overbearing women. She'd be fine if she was just less…Hannah.

He hadn't wanted her when she was being herself. And that stung more than it ought to. The nickname Oaklee had called her—the General—actually hurt. She knew people found her intimidating. She tried as hard as she could not to let it get to her, but sometimes, the loneliness crept in. Particularly when her best friends were all in happy relationships, moving through the world in couples, and she was on the outside looking in. According to Liam, the ex, no one would ever want a woman who was so determined to wear the pants.

Hannah was always the third wheel, and she smiled her way through it. Maybe no one would ever want someone like her, like Liam said. But she'd rather be alone than be less of herself.

"So what is keeping you busy these days?" Cam asked, seemingly more at ease than she was. "What's the real estate market like?"

"It's a bit of a buyer's market at the moment," she answered and then lifted her cup and took a sip of her coffee. "You looking to buy?"

He shook his head. "Honestly? This concussion has thrown me more than I expected. I need to get back on the ice, but I'm afraid to be sidelined. There's always that little bit of fear that the next time will be a career ender. Plus, I've got two years left on my contract. Who knows if I'll be traded or find myself a free agent in that time? I've got a condo, but I could be in another city, you know? Looking at a permanent house isn't really in the cards right now."

At least Darling was her home. She didn't have to feel as if her life were…transient. Or in the hands of someone else.

"But you're happy?" she asked, curious.

"Not happy about being scratched from the lineup,

that's for sure." The café had gotten busier, and she noticed Cam wincing now and again.

"Is the noise getting to you?"

"I wish I could say no, but I do seem to be more sensitive to light and sound. I only have the odd dizziness or woozy feelings, but I'm not headache free yet."

"I'm sorry. That's got to be frustrating." She wrapped up the third of her sandwich that was left and tucked it in the bag. He'd finished his eggs and had one little sausage link left. She realized she hadn't even broached the topic of the benefit yet, and this was the perfect time.

"So if you happen to be at loose ends while you're home, we have this charity thing going on just before Christmas. A literacy event. This is the second year, and all the proceeds go to local literacy programs. You want to help out?"

"What kind of charity thing?"

Hannah took advantage of the question to press forward. "It's a community day of literacy. There are events all over town. Participants can grab a bookmark and get it stamped at each shop, with a draw at the end. The library has a special reading and a used-book sale, and in the evening, there's a ticketed dinner and silent auction."

He raised his eyebrows. "Sounds ambitious."

"Last year, we raised over ten thousand dollars. Corporate donations took us to just shy of twenty." She was proud of that number, considering it had been their first year, and they'd been trying everything for the first time. Darling wasn't a large town, and twenty thousand had helped a lot of kids learn to read.

She folded her hands on the table and looked him straight in the face, trying to ignore how handsome he was. He had such great hair and perfect teeth. Was it possible for a hockey player to have teeth that great, she wondered? His last contract had been in the millions, double digit millions. Twenty grand must seem like a drop in the bucket to him. But to the organizations nearby, it meant resources for tons of kids.

"Will you help out? You saw that kid this morning. Having a local hero like you would be a huge draw. You could read a story at the library and then maybe speak at the dinner. It would guarantee a sell-out crowd."

"You want me to read a book to some kids?" His voice cooled, and he sat back in his chair a bit.

"Well, yes. I know you're not an author, but I'm sure we could find you a great hockey story to share."

His face flattened ever so slightly into a polite veneer. "Have you been waiting for the right opportunity to ask me about this?"

Hannah blushed a little and gave a small shrug. "Sort of. We just found out yesterday that our headlining author has to have surgery and backed out. We could really use your help."

He sighed, and her heart sank. He was not pleased, she could tell. His gaze had darkened, and his full lips were now a flat line.

"Look, I wish you luck, but I came home to recover and enjoy the holiday. Have some privacy. Not find myself in the middle of some big event."

"It would only be one day," she reasoned, desperate for him to change his mind.

"Sure, but I can't even sit in a café without my head reacting. A library full of screaming kids? I'm sorry, Hannah. The answer is no."

Hannah felt the solution slipping through her fingers and leaned forward. "Look, Cam, I know this looks like we're using you for your celebrity, and you're not wrong. But you're a hometown guy, and it's such a good cause. Please help us." She hated sounding desperate, but finding someone willing to come to their little town just before Christmas with so little notice? They'd had the previous plans in place for months.

"I'm sorry, I can't. I'll give you something for the auction. A signed jersey or something."

"Can't, or won't?"

She could have bitten her tongue. Her earlier jitters had fled in the face of his refusal, because she'd seriously thought he'd say yes. She knew for a fact he'd supported charities in the past. Like the one providing sports equipment to underprivileged kids.

But he wouldn't help out the town that had supported him, and frankly, she was disappointed in him.

Her face must have showed it, because he shook his head a little. "You're looking at me like my grandma used to when I lied about taking cookies out of the Tupperware in her cupboard. I'm sorry, Hannah, but I came home to rest. Doctor's orders. And to enjoy the holiday, too. I want to keep a low profile." He toyed with his napkin. "The sooner I recover, the sooner I'm back on the ice. Maybe you don't understand how many requests I get. I need a break."

It wasn't like reading a stupid storybook would set his recovery back, but Hannah knew she wasn't going to get anywhere with him today. She pushed her chair back and stood. "Well, that's that, I guess. I'd better get back to work."

Cam stood, too, surprising Hannah, who hadn't expected the old-fashioned courtesy. "I'm sorry to disappoint you, Hannah. More sorry than you know."

Was he? Was he really? She felt as if the words were mere lip service, so she offered a weak smile. "Have a good day. I hope you get some rest." She couldn't resist adding the last barb. Suddenly, his good looks didn't seem so attractive anymore. Even if he'd been open to the idea in a small way, they would have had somewhere to go with it. But that had been a definitive shut down.

She dropped her garbage in the trash can on the way by, heading straight for the door before Willow could catch her and quiz her on what had happened at breakfast with Cam. Willow and Laurel had been nagging her about her love life more lately, and she really didn't need the curiosity. She and Cam were not going to be a thing.

It wasn't that she didn't understand wanting to spend a low-key Christmas to recover from his concussion. She wasn't entirely unsympathetic. He just had to see what a great event it was and how many kids could benefit. But it wasn't in her nature to give up on what she really wanted. It was what made her a good Realtor and businesswoman.

She went back into her office, sat in her chair, and rolled up to her desk, reaching for her keyboard.

Maybe if Cam saw the numbers, he'd be more inclined to help. Because the last thing this event needed was Hannah reading to kids. There was nothing exciting or special about that.

Absolutely nothing.

3

Cam decided to get some fresh air after the encounter with Hannah, so he left The Purple Pig and made his way down Main, trying to inhale slow, deep breaths. His pulse still pattered at his throat, a result of the anxiety he'd felt the moment Hannah had made her request. There was no way he could sit in front of a crowd of kids and read out loud to them. Not an ice cube's chance in hell. He could just see it now. A group of children all starry-eyed at the big hockey star, only to realize how unheroic he was when he started stumbling over the words or reading too slowly.

Hannah had no idea what she was asking, and he wasn't about to tell her. Besides, he hadn't lied. He really was home to recuperate and spend the holiday with his family.

Even he knew that was a technicality. He'd said no because reading was a gigantic struggle for him, and nothing he would ever do in public.

He'd gone exactly a block and a half when he heard his name being called. When he turned, Oaklee was bearing down on him, presumably on her way to work. Damn, this town really was small.

"Good morning," he said, waiting for her to catch up.

Oaklee stopped and stared up at him. "What's wrong with you?"

"What do you mean?"

"You look like a constipated bear. What put you in a bad mood? Or is your head hurting?"

Why had he thought coming home was a good idea?

Oaklee didn't know about his *problem*. No one did, and he wanted to keep it that way.

"I'm just tired, Oaklee. If you haven't had a concussion, you probably don't get it."

"Then why are you out here?"

He started walking again, toward town hall, where she worked. "I wanted some fresh air."

"So you went to the café?" She nodded at his to-go cup and his rapidly cooling coffee.

"What's with the third degree?" he asked, his teeth grinding to the sound of her heeled boots clicking on the sidewalk as she kept up with him. Funny how certain noises seemed to set him on edge. "Yes, I went and had breakfast. With Hannah, actually."

"Oh! Did she ask you about the benefit?"

Cam stopped in the middle of the sidewalk and stared at his little sister as it all became clear. "Damn. Did you put her up to that?"

"It might have been my idea. She was majorly

stressed about it yesterday. So you're going to do it, right?"

"No, I'm not. I'll donate something, but I'm not going to replace whatever author you were supposed to have."

Oaklee put her hand on his arm. "Bro. This is not cool."

He loved his sister. He did. So he was as gentle as possible when he answered, "Neither is setting me up to do something I'm not comfortable with, Oaklee. I would hope you'd understand that."

"I understand that you could have given Hannah thirty minutes of your time on a Saturday, and instead, you probably offered a jersey. It's not like you, Cam."

Her eyes were soft with concern rather than censure, and he let out a sigh. "Maybe coming home was a mistake."

She linked her arm through his and they started walking again. "Why would you say that? Mom and Dad are thrilled. And so am I. I don't see enough of my big brother."

He didn't know how to phrase his discontent without sounding spoiled and privileged. "It's just...everywhere I go, people generally want something. And it's not a bad thing. I know I'm blessed. I appreciate my fans, I really do. At the same time, I miss being a regular guy. I kind of thought I'd have that opportunity at home, you know? And I'm home less than twenty-four hours and already someone wants something."

Her lips lifted in a smile. "Waaah, waaah."

Cam chuckled. He knew better than to give his little

sister a pity story. One of the things he liked about her was that she didn't take his crap. It still blew him away that she and his best friend were seriously in love.

"I know, it's a tough life I lead."

"Please, just think about it?"

"Oaklee, let it drop, okay? I'll donate, but I'm not doing some story time at the library. Now, aren't you late for work?" he asked, lifting an eyebrow as he glanced down at her.

"Yeah, I guess." Oaklee was pouting now.

"You might be able to get around Mom and Dad with that look, but it's never worked on me. Put your lip away."

She laughed then, and he felt some of the tension dissolve between them. He walked her to the parking lot of town hall and watched as she headed inside. His baby sister was all grown up. Of course, he'd known that already, but it was strange seeing her here with her own place and a job and a relationship... So many things had changed since he left, and yet they'd stayed the same, too.

The walk had done him good, so he headed back to where he'd parked by the café. The air had a crisp bite to it as he shrugged his shoulders and looked at the other storefronts in the building. Next to The Purple Pig was a yoga studio, and next to that, Darling Realty. Hannah's office.

Hannah, with that Gallagher red hair and eyes that seemed to see right into his solar plexus. Not to mention the rockin' bod she had going on. She had legs for miles in those boots today, and that dress... It had hugged every lean curve. She'd been older than him in school, but she'd always been hot. Rory would kill him for saying so, but he'd always had kind of a thing for Hannah. And not just her looks, either. She had zero tolerance for bullshit and had never dated dumbasses. Particular and discriminating, that was Hannah.

He wondered if he met any of her criteria now that he was older and a lot more successful than he'd been back then. If his money made him less of a dumb jock in her eyes.

Oaklee was right about one thing. It was a good cause, and so he went to the Darling Realty door and opened it, stepping out of the cold and into the warmth. He didn't like how he'd left things with Hannah this morning, and during his walk, he'd come up with a way to help her and ease his conscience at the same time.

"Can I help you?" The receptionist looked up and her mouth fell open. "Oh my God. You're Cam Collier."

He smiled his standard smile and nodded. "That's right. Is Hannah in?"

She nodded quickly, her eyes wide. "I'll just go get her. Hang on."

He waited as she scurried away and took the opportunity to look around the reception area. It was very Hannah, dressed up with lovely touches but very clean and efficient looking. A gentle gray covered the walls, with prints featuring Darling landmarks scattered strategically. The reception area chairs were darker gray, and there was not a thing out of place at the receptionist's desk. It was both professional and welcoming, and he liked it a lot.

"Cam?" Hannah entered the area, a frown etching her brows. "What's up?" Her eyes lit up, and she smiled. "Have you reconsidered?"

"About the library? No. But I went for a walk and came up with an idea."

She was disappointed, he could tell. Her shoulders drooped a little when he said no, and her smile dimmed a bit. He didn't like disappointing her, he discovered. But worse than that would be the look on her face when she realized he was exactly the wrong person to be reading in front of a crowd. He did have one thing to offer, though.

"Come on into my office, then." She looked over at the receptionist, who was still staring. "Sheila, if anyone calls, I'm unavailable, okay?"

"The house inspection for Jim Hernandez is due in today. And we're waiting for a counteroffer from the Bajwas."

"I won't be long." She beckoned to Cam. "Come on in, Cam."

He followed her into her office and took a breath as she shut the door behind him.

There were windows on one wall, with slatted blinds that were open enough to let in the morning light but still retain privacy. Her office reflected the reception area, with those restful grays and beautiful prints. But there was more of Hannah in here, too. Fresh flowers on the credenza. A laptop open on her desk, and what looked like a day planner. And a coffee mug that proudly proclaimed, *Realtor…because Bad Ass isn't an official job title.*

"Nice mug."

"Thanks. Santa put it in my stocking a few years ago."

He tried to imagine her in fuzzy pajamas, opening a Christmas stocking, and he found the image more alluring than he ought to. Hannah was always put together. Thinking of her soft and mussed from sleep did something to him that he wasn't sure he liked. Or maybe he liked it a little too much.

"So," she said, leaning back against her desk. "What's your idea? I was just running some numbers on the benefit, actually. Both expenses and then where the funds go and how many children it helps." She reached behind her for a sheaf of papers and handed it over.

He took them and scanned the sheets, pretending to read them. It wasn't that he couldn't. It was just that he'd have to sit down and really work his way through so things weren't jumbled. He cleared his mind and forced his thoughts back to the matter at hand. "I appreciate you printing this out, but just tell me straight. How much do you need financially to make this a success? I can help there. I'll donate to the auction, and I'll underwrite any expenses you incur."

She stilled. "You want to underwrite the benefit."

Hannah stared at Cam and didn't know what to say. On one hand, the offer was very generous, particularly since all their communication and promotion had to be redone—without Jillian's name and face on it. On the other hand, he was throwing money at the issue rather than giving of himself.

She must have hesitated too long, because he took a step forward and put the papers back on her desk. "I'll make a donation, too, of course."

"A donation," she parroted.

"It's not that I don't think it's a good cause. I do, of course I do!" He put his hands into the back pockets of his jeans. "I just want to be in the background. Out of the spotlight."

She wavered. While having him read at the library and perhaps speak at the dinner would be amazing, she also respected that he wanted some privacy. This morning had been proof enough that he was recognized wherever he went. As cute as the little boy had been, it had interrupted his breakfast. And yet he'd been lovely and gracious. She wasn't sure why he was so hesitant to participate, but she was smart enough to not look a gift horse in the mouth.

"I appreciate the funds, of course," she said quietly, meeting his eyes. "But we won't have much of an event if we don't have someone special lined up."

"I'm sure if you explain about the cancellation, people will understand."

They probably would. But Hannah would still feel as if she'd failed.

She sighed. There was still time. There was a chance she could find someone, right? Someone who was not Cam?

Someone who was not over six feet of sexiness that

made her lose her focus the moment he stared into her eyes, imploring her to understand?

She knew what Willow would say about this new fixation on Cam. Willow would say she needed to get laid. And Willow might not be entirely wrong. It had been a very long time. So long she wouldn't own to it if asked.

"Hey," he said softly, coming forward. "I have my reasons, Hannah. Please don't be mad." A lopsided grin flickered on his lips. "If I remember right, an angry Hannah Gallagher is a fearsome thing."

She couldn't help it. She laughed. He looked so innocent and cute right now as he teased her. He'd always been able to do that, she realized. Even when he was a kid. She'd be annoyed at him and Rory, and he'd flash her a grin that melted away her frustration. Not that she'd ever let on. He'd always had charisma. Some of it was cocky, but mostly it was just a natural thing that was hard to resist.

Like right now.

"I know you have your reasons. And to be honest, you shouldn't have to justify anything to me. I'm just disappointed is all."

"I don't like disappointing you."

"If I remember right, you don't like disappointing anyone."

Silence fell between them as he stared at her. Maybe he didn't expect her to see him so clearly, but there were things they had in common. Drive, for one. He couldn't have made it where he was now without it. And a need for approval. She'd watched him look up into the stands for his parents during every peewee game. Heard the interviews where he'd confessed to letting his team down or the fans.

Neither of them liked to fail. It suddenly dawned on her that this trip home must, in some way, feel like a failure. He was away from his job, away from his team, forced to recover. Did it make him feel weak? Heck, she was an amateur athlete, doing half marathons and, last fall, her first half Ironman. And she knew how frustrated she'd gotten when she had to step back from training with an injury. This was his career. He was the team captain. Totally different thing.

"Sorry," she said quietly. "I didn't mean to say that."

"You're not wrong," he answered. "I don't like disappointing you, either. So will you believe me when I say that I've said no for a good reason?"

She nodded. There were things he wasn't saying, but a lot that he was, and she appreciated that.

"Thank you, Cam." She pushed away from the desk and went to stand before him. "For coming to see me and explaining, and for your offer to help. I accept."

She held out her hand for him to shake, and he folded her fingers inside his larger, warm hand. He held on for longer than was proper, while his dark gaze delved into hers.

And then he did the last thing Hannah expected. He tugged on her hand, pulled her closer, and kissed her.

Every rational thought skittered out of her brain at the first contact of his mouth on hers. His lips were soft and yet firm as they moved over her mouth. She let out a little sigh and melted against him. His arm came around her and pulled her against his bomber jacket. It smelled of leather and fresh air and whatever cologne he'd put on that morning—something deliciously fresh and manly that made her want to lick his neck.

He was kissing her, and she was thinking of licking his neck. What kind of madness was this? And yet she was helpless to stop. He was an exceptionally good kisser. Firm when he needed to be, gentle and teasing in between, and always, always in control. She loved that, she realized, as he cupped the side of her face with a wide palm and took the kiss deeper. It was sheer bliss to let him command the kiss and for her to just follow.

When their breath labored and the kiss turned a bit wild, Hannah stepped back, shocked at how quickly they'd gone from a handshake to sucking face in her office. Her office, for Pete's sake! Her chest rose and fell with panting breaths, and every part of her tingled with arousal.

"Wow," Cam said, running a hand through his hair. His breathing was ragged, too, and one quick glance at his jeans told her she wasn't alone in the arousal department.

She had to get a hold of herself. "I can honestly say that is the first time I've ever sealed a bargain in that manner."

"It was definitely…unexpected."

"Unexpected? You kissed me."

"Yeah, but I didn't imagine it would be like that." His dark gaze seared her now. "Damn, Hannah. Just… damn." His eyes twinkled at her. "I've wanted to do that since I was thirteen. If I'd known you could kiss like that, I would have done it much sooner."

She shouldn't be flattered, but she'd heard so much criticism in the past that she drank up the praise like she was parched in the desert and it was life-giving water.

"I'm as surprised as you are," she replied, smoothing her hands down her dress.

"Have dinner with me," he said. He'd regained his composure and channeled the cockiness she remembered so well. "Tonight."

He didn't have to say the words for her to know that he wasn't just asking her to dinner. And despite the chemistry that clearly sparked between them, she was not the type to throw caution to the wind and have a fling.

What was more, he knew it.

"I think I'll pass," she replied, hearing the regret in the words but standing by them anyway. "This isn't a good idea, Cam."

"Are you sure? Because it felt like a very good idea about two minutes ago."

"We both know you're not asking me out to dinner. Or at least, not just dinner. And I'm not prepared for anything more than that."

It hurt just to say the words. Because Hannah got the idea that being with Cam would be something spectacular.

He stepped back a little. "Then I'll just say if you ever change your mind…"

It was tempting. So very tempting. She desperately wanted to say yes. But sex… It was something Hannah took very seriously. There had to be emotions involved, and a genuine caring. Maybe not exactly love, but close to it. It was how she was built. And after years of being criticized, both in the bedroom and out, she didn't let herself be vulnerable like that very often.

"Thank you, Cam."

"You're welcome."

He let himself out, though she heard him stop at the desk and say something to Sheila, who giggled in response. Hannah smiled to herself. He was such a charmer, and he knew it. And yet it wasn't insincere.

And he kissed like the devil. She put her fingers to her lips and sighed. His invitation was more tempting than he knew. But Hannah wasn't sure she could take one more hit to her pride. The thought of being with Cam and him finding her wanting was more than she could bear.

4

Cam didn't see Hannah for the rest of the week. He did as he was supposed to and took lots of down time. He monitored his symptoms and was pleased with how they seemed to be disappearing, though he knew he had to be symptom free for several days before he would even be cleared for basic workouts. He ventured into town and did some holiday shopping, and then into Burlington where there was a wider selection. This Christmas was different. Normally, he shipped gifts to the family, but this year he was going to be here. He intended to purchase them all and wrap them himself, too.

He also kept himself glued to the sports channel and what was happening with the league. He missed team meetings and being in the locker room. He got lots of emails, but reading them was onerous.

Replying was just as difficult.

He was sitting on the back deck, having coffee and

enjoying the brisk air, when he heard the fence gate open. "Hey, you out here?"

Rory. Cam smiled and called out, "Yeah, on the deck. Come on up and have a seat."

Rory was the best friend Cam had ever had, and he'd missed him a lot when he went away to play major junior. Rory had been charged with watching out for Oaklee. He'd also been game for anything when Cam had been home in the off-season. It was the one friendship from his youth that had sustained. And yet Rory didn't know Cam's secret, either. Normally, it didn't bother Cam as much as it did now. He'd developed ways of hiding his disability. And though he'd never been formally tested, he was pretty sure that his reading and writing issues were because he had dyslexia.

Rory climbed the few steps to the deck and shook his head as he stared at Cam. "Seriously, it's cold as balls out here. Why are you on the deck?"

"I miss the ice." Cam grinned at his friend and took a sip of his coffee. "You want a coffee? I can make you one."

"Naw, I'm good. I had coffee with Oaklee before work today, and another with Ethan when he stopped over to stash the boys' gifts in my garage. If I have a third, I'll be spinning around like the Tasmanian Devil."

"Ethan's boys are getting big."

"Yep. New toboggans for Christmas, and a hockey net for the front yard. Kind of difficult to hide those away from curious boys."

Rory sat in the chair beside Cam and grimaced as the cold surface greeted his butt. "Dude. My grandmother would tell me I'll get hemorrhoids from sitting on something this cold."

"Wuss," Cam replied. "So what brings you over?"

"I don't work until two. And there's something I want to talk to you about."

Cam drank the last of his coffee and gave Rory a skeptical look. "If you're here to plead the case for the literacy benefit—"

"No. Not that Oaklee didn't ask, but I said no way am I getting in the middle of that. That's not it."

Rory's smile had disappeared, and he shifted on his chair. Cam frowned. He hoped this wasn't anything to do with Oaklee. Rory was his best friend, but if he hurt Oaklee, Cam might just have to knock him into next week.

"What's going on?"

"Well, the thing is…you're her brother, and you're my best friend, and I kinda feel like I need to talk to you before I…" His voice trailed away and then he straightened. "Before I ask her to marry me."

Cam wanted to grin from ear to ear, but he figured it would be fun to make Rory sweat a little. "You're asking my permission?"

"Not exactly. But I think I need your blessing."

Cam crossed an ankle over his knee and looked up at the cloudless sky. "Huh. You didn't ask for my blessing before taking her to bed, as I remember."

"Jesus, Cam," Rory blurted out, giving Cam some perverse satisfaction. What was the point of having a best friend if you couldn't give him some shit now and again?

Cam looked over at Rory and chuckled. "Just sayin', bro. Hell, you guys have been together over a year and are living together. Nothing I say would make a difference, nor should it. She loves you. You love her."

The look on Rory's face was so relieved it was comical, so Cam added, "But if you ever hurt her, I'll crush you. Got it?"

"You and what army, invalid?"

Oh, trash talk. Cam's favorite thing. He lifted an eyebrow. "Have you seen my teammates?"

Rory met his raised eyebrow with one of his own. "Have you met my brothers?"

They both laughed, and Cam held out a hand. Rory shook it and there was a moment of something between them, of friendship and respect and affection that had never wavered over the years. "Hey. If you guys get married, that'll make us brothers, too. Congratulations, Rory. I'm happy for you both."

"Thanks. Hopefully, your dad will feel the same."

"God, you really are old-fashioned. And my parents love you. When are you planning to pop the question?"

"Just before Christmas. I don't want to do it Christmas morning. And if I do it before the holiday, she won't expect it."

"You've got it all figured out."

Rory shrugged. "Everything has pretty much fallen into place since Oaklee and I decided to make this into a relationship. Before it was just—" He stopped talking, and his ruddy cheeks turned even more red. "Uh…"

"Hooking up," Cam said mildly. "Excuse me while I try to erase that picture from my mind."

"Yeah, well, you should try it sometime. Your single status is kind of legendary."

Cam got up from his chair. "I'm going to make another coffee. There's decaf if you don't want to be wired. Mom says that caffeine gives her hot flashes." He grinned. "So does red wine, but she hasn't stopped drinking that."

They went inside, and Cam made more coffee. The house was empty, and he thought about how much cozier it was than his condo. Living alone was good in some ways but lonely in others. Just seeing a dirty plate and knife in the sink from his dad's morning toast was kind of nice.

As the coffee brewed, Rory unfortunately picked up where he'd left off. Cam's single status.

"So you're not dating anyone?"

"Not at the moment." He went to the fridge to get milk, wondering what Rory would say if Cam admitted he was thinking about "hooking up" with Hannah. He wasn't sure Rory would be as magnanimous about it as Cam had been about Oaklee.

"Dude," Rory said, in a tone that made Cam chuckle. "Back in the day we…well, you know. Neither of us had a shortage of dates. But these days we never hear of you dating anyone. Are you okay?"

God, he'd missed Rory. There was nothing but utter concern in Rory's last question, and it was a balm to realize that despite the years and miles between them, their childhood bond was still strong.

"I'm just really private," he assured Rory. "And to be honest, I don't know if I want to try to have a serious relationship when I could move around at any time, you know? And even when I'm in one place, there's so much season travel. It's a lot to ask of a partner."

It wasn't like he hadn't tried it once. He had. With a sweet girl named Alyssa. It was the one and only time he'd truly been in love. But after a few months of new-relationship bliss, a strange vibe had developed in their relationship. Alyssa hated when he was gone on the road with the team all the time, and she got really sideways over girls hanging around the locker room. Cam, for all his flirting, was not the kind of man to mess around with random women, and certainly not when he really cared about someone else.

That had been when he was in Boston. When he got traded to Denver, that was it. Alyssa had broken it off. She'd been finishing school, and they'd both known that trying to keep something going long distance was asking for trouble. If she didn't like him doing away games, how would she handle him living in an entirely different state? The jealousy and arguments had ended up killing their relationship more than any mid-season trade.

"Maybe you just haven't met the right one yet."

"Maybe," he answered.

They took their coffee into the living room and moved on to other subjects, but Cam couldn't get the kiss with Hannah off his mind. He couldn't offer anything long term, and she wasn't into hookups. And that left them exactly nowhere. Whatever attraction they had for each other was going to go unexplored. And that, he realized, was a crying shame.

HANNAH TUGGED HER WHITE KNITTED HAT OVER HER hair and gave a last look in her hall mirror. Two inches of snow had fallen this morning, which made it absolutely perfect for the tree lighting tonight. But it also meant bundling up in hat and mittens for the occasion. With one last adjustment of her jacket, she tucked her phone in her jeans pocket and headed out the door to make the walk to the Green and the huge tree set up near the Kissing Bridge.

It was already dark, and Hannah let out a happy sigh, taking in the lights decorating each house and yard. Inflatable snowmen and Santas waved happily in the breeze, and eaves and shrubs were decorated with glowing bulbs of various colors. There was foot traffic, too, as the lighting was guaranteed to bring out a good crowd. Indeed, by the time she made it to the park, all the nearby parking spots were occupied, and a throng had gathered.

A church group had set up a hot chocolate and cookie station, raising money for their Christmas adopt-a-family. The high school choir was also lining up in rows to lead the caroling. Hannah stood back for a moment and simply watched, her heart full. Darling was home, and while it had its faults, right now, it was the perfect place to be.

She spied her family at a distance. They were to the left of the tree, gathered in a group, with her mom and dad at the center. Ethan and Willow were there with the two boys running around everyone, and Brenna was bundled under blankets in a stroller. Aiden and Lauren were also there with a nearly identical stroller holding a sleeping Maggie, and the twins, Claire and Cait, were handing out cookies. Hannah stayed on the outside, ever conscious that she was the oldest and single. Loved but sometimes not quite fitting in.

And no one to blame for it but herself. She was the one letting her feelings hold her back, and she knew it.

As she watched, Rory and Oaklee joined the Gallagher clan. Her throat tightened as she realized everyone looked so content. Meanwhile, she was lonely. Not that she ever showed it or would ever say such a thing. Not Hannah Gallagher, the General, the power-through woman who made mountains move.

"You're not with the others. How come?"

Cam's smooth baritone voice sent shivers up her spine, and she turned to face him. "Oh. Well, I just got here."

He seemed to accept her answer and smiled. "This is just like I remember it. It's comforting that some things don't change, isn't it?"

Was it? She loved this place and this moment, but would she be doing this every December for the rest of her life? She might like to have a change at some point. Some…adventure. A challenge or two.

"The snow makes everything perfect," she said instead. "When they turn on the lights, it's going to be gorgeous."

"Do you want to join the others?"

She shrugged. "I don't know. Who are you hanging with?"

"Right now, you. Mom and Dad decided to stay home. Mom's got a cold, and Dad's fussing. It's kind of cute."

"I'm sure my family wouldn't mind you joining in. If you want to."

His gaze plumbed hers. "Sure, why not?"

They made their way over to the Gallaghers and were separated by conversation and excited children bobbing about. Oaklee got Cam a hot chocolate; Hannah took a turn holding Brenna and adoring her sweet little face. She loved being an auntie. After Ethan's first wife died, she'd pitched in to help with childcare while Ethan went back to work. Now, she couldn't wait for the baby girls to get big enough so she could take them on outings and spoil them rotten.

Shopping trips and girly nights with Fun Auntie Hannah were going to be a thing.

When Brenna started fussing, she gave the baby back to Willow and stood back, waiting for the tree to be lit. As the mayor grabbed a microphone to make a brief speech, it seemed as though the family units all clustered together. Even the twins stayed beside each other, leaving Hannah and Cam on the fringes. His arm came around her, holding a steaming cup of chocolate. "You didn't get any," he murmured.

"Thanks." She tried not to be affected by the observation and the remedy. It was considerate of him, and she was glad to have him at her shoulder. The eyes of the town were on him, she could tell. And why not? He was their hometown boy, their very own celebrity, attending a long-standing Christmas tradition.

"Seen with me twice," she whispered. "That's how rumors start."

"Meh. They start anyway. At least this way, I have someone to stand with. Everyone else in my life is paired up. It's weird."

She snorted. "Tell me about it."

"Is it still a rumor if it's true?"

"Nice try, Collier. Still not going to *dinner* with you."

He tried not to laugh and started coughing instead, earning him some curious looks. But then the choir started the first carol, and the crowd started to sing along with "Jingle Bells".

One carol followed another. Hannah sang along softly; she had a decent voice and adored holiday music. To her surprise, Cam's deeper voice joined in a few times, too, and she felt an unexpected kinship to him. His body was just behind hers, close enough she could sense the size and warmth of him, close enough she wanted to lean back and discover what it would be like to rest in his embrace. Instead, she stayed still, listening to his slightly off-key singing.

She did not want to like him. She didn't want him to be nice. That was what was going to get her into trouble, wasn't it?

When the caroling was over, and her hot chocolate long gone, he put his hand on the small of her back. "Do you want company on the walk home?"

"As long as you understand it's just a walk home."

His eyes glittered, and that silly smile flirted with his mouth. "Of course."

They said their goodbyes, and everyone scattered.

Hannah was sure people noticed them walking off together, but it would never be possible to go anywhere with Cam and be invisible. It was a simple walk home in the snow. Nothing more.

They didn't say anything during the walk, not until they were climbing the hill on her street.

"How's the head?" she asked.

He sighed. "Okay. I had an appointment yesterday in Boston. Every time a symptom returns, I have to set the clock back. But right now, I've been symptom free for five days. I can start light exercise. Go me."

She laughed. "What do you consider light exercise?"

"Well, I'm going to start with my morning run again and hope for the best. I've been going squirrely."

"If you want company, let me know. I run most mornings."

She didn't know what had possessed her to invite herself, but it was out there now. Besides, there was something alluring about the idea of running alongside Cam. She was a physical person but didn't often have a partner to share that with. There was Willow, but she was into yoga rather than triathlons.

Their steps slowed a little. "I might do that," he said. "It's nice having a workout buddy."

They reached her house and paused on the sidewalk. "Thank you for the walk home, Cam."

Their eyes met, and that delicious feeling wound its way through her body again. "Don't," she whispered. "Not in the middle of my street."

"Don't worry," he responded, his voice low and

sultry. "After the other day, I know better than to kiss you in public. The tree won't be the only thing lit up."

Her lips twitched despite her struggle to remain firm. "I'm not inviting you in."

"Okay."

She stared at him for a minute, until he shrugged. "Han, when a woman says she's not interested, that's it. I don't push."

Her mouth dropped open at his honesty, and she appreciated him so much more. They both knew it wasn't because she wasn't interested. But she'd set boundaries, and he was honoring them. Damned if that wasn't sexy.

"I don't need to," he added with that silly smile curving his lips. The moment turned light again as she rolled her eyes and let out a skeptical breath.

"Bunnies lined up around the rink, huh?"

"Sure." He winked at her. But then his gaze turned dark and serious again. "But you know they're not there for me."

She frowned, her brows knitting together. "What do you mean?"

"They're there for who they think I am. They're there for the guy they see at center ice and on the sports interviews and the replays on the TV. I know that. Which is why I don't go home with bunnies."

Hannah was impressed, by both his actions and his insight. She'd never thought of it before, but that kind of life sounded rather lonely.

She was tempted to ask him in anyway, for a drink or something, but she wasn't sure if he was allowed alcohol right now. She was also a little afraid he'd misinterpret her intentions, so she kept the thought to herself.

"You're surprised," he said, shoving his hands in his pockets.

"Yes and no. You ate that stuff up when you were a kid, at least if Rory is to be believed. But what teenage boy wouldn't? You've outgrown that kind of thing, I think."

"Thank you," he replied quietly. "I've tried."

Silence fell again, and the snow started up, too, so that big, fat flakes floated down around them.

"Listen," she whispered, closing her eyes and tilting her head to the sky. "You can hear the snow fall."

The delicate shush of the flakes filled the air around them. Hannah opened her eyes and saw that he'd closed his eyes and was listening, too, and her heart did this strange little flip, seeing his long lashes resting on the hollows beneath his eyes, and how the flakes settled on his hair.

Uh oh.

He opened his eyes and caught her staring at him. "Hannah. Let me walk you to your door. Because I'm going to kiss you goodnight, but not here in the middle of the sidewalk."

Now her pulse was really thumping, and her stomach was doing somersaults. She felt about fifteen, when she'd had a crush on Ben Fraser, and he'd reached over on the school bus and held her hand.

She led the way up the walk to her front door, inserted the key with a surprisingly steady hand, and went inside. He followed and shut the door behind him.

Yet he stayed there, with his back to the door, not venturing farther.

"If you don't want me to kiss you, say so," he murmured, his soft voice riding along her nerve endings.

She wanted a lot more than a kiss but was afraid to admit it, afraid to take that step. She swallowed, trying to sort out what to say, when he took a step forward, cupped her face in his hands, and planted the sweetest ever kiss on her surprised lips.

It wasn't like the other day in her office. He only lingered a few seconds and then was gone again, leaving her lips tingling and wondering what had just happened. It was simple and rather chaste and utterly wonderful.

"Goodnight, Hannah Banana," he whispered, and before she could say another word, he was out the door and leaving footprints on the snow gathering on her walk.

5

Hannah didn't know what to make of that kiss. She laced up her sneakers and pulled on her hat before heading out the door. Maybe a good run would clear her thoughts.

The temperature hovered at about twenty-five degrees, not too cold, and she started down the hill at a warm-up pace. Twice now, Cam had kissed her. He hadn't pushed either time, hadn't asked for more than she could give. She appreciated that. The problem was, she wanted more. It surprised her to realize it, but it had been over three years since she'd even contemplated a relationship. Liam hadn't wanted to stay with someone who had to "control everything." Hannah knew she was a lot. She was a strong personality and had always been a high achiever. But she was tired of apologizing for it. More than that, she'd often wondered if Liam's remarks had been designed to cut her where she was most vulnerable, because he didn't want to be with a woman stronger than he was.

Maybe that was unfair. Maybe not. But Cam's comment about fans hanging around for the person they thought he was had struck a chord. People had this idea of who Hannah Gallagher was, but they'd be surprised to know she had insecurities and weaknesses same as everyone else. Feelings. Needs and wants.

She went down Main and diverted from her usual route to head toward the suburbs on the north side of town, where the Colliers lived. She wasn't up this way often, but it was a pretty area of town, and older than the newer subdivisions. Tidy houses and neat yards were punctuated with mature trees. Most of her clients were after new builds, but she loved showing these older properties. They weren't as flashy, but they held a permanence and history that the other new houses didn't.

She went through the intersection where the entrance to the neighborhood met the main road and started down the other side. It would curve around town and come back along Fisher Creek, where she could either head back home or cross the bridge to the golf course. She'd only gone maybe forty yards when a voice called out behind her. "Hey, Han! Han, wait up!"

She kept her feet moving as she turned around and saw Cam coming toward her, dressed in sneakers, sweats, a hat with his team's logo on it, and a fleece jacket. He looked so good, and not like he should be on anyone's injured list. He caught up with her easily, and she didn't make a fuss. She just started running again, and he kept pace.

"Fancy meeting you here," she said dryly, and Cam laughed.

"I told you I was going to start running. Is this your normal route?"

She could lie and say yes. Instead, she said, "No, but I felt like something different to clear my mind this morning."

"Oh." A few seconds passed with nothing but the sound of their feet hitting the concrete sidewalk. Then he added, "What do you need to clear it of?"

Hannah glanced up at him and decided that being honest and blunt had served her fairly well throughout her life, so there was no reason to be different now. "You, actually."

"I'm glad to hear it. I couldn't stop thinking of you last night, either."

Well, damn.

They ran in peace for a while longer, to the main part of town and toward the bridge. Their breath came easily, the respiration of two people in good shape who enjoyed the exercise.

Hannah spoke next, as if the conversation had never broken off. "The thing is, I'm not quite sure why you've kissed me. Twice."

"Um, it's kind of obvious, Hannah. Didn't I tell you you're hot? I kissed you because I wanted to. I'm assuming you kissed me back because you wanted to, too."

He wasn't making this any easier.

"I mean, what do you plan to get out of this? Where do you see this going?"

He was prevented from answering for a few moments as someone in a car honked, and he lifted a hand in a wave. They crossed the bridge and turned right, heading toward the golf course.

"So," he started, speaking between breaths. "You want to know what my intentions are. Why start something when I'm only here for a few weeks."

"Well, yes."

"I haven't really thought about it. But you're different from me, so you're looking at all the angles. Wondering how the pieces fit together."

She didn't answer. He was a hundred percent right.

"Look, Hannah, I head back to Denver after the holidays. My career is there. Maybe I'll stay there, maybe I'll get traded. I really don't know what the future holds. That's why I don't do relationships. During the season, I'm in one city after another. If we make the playoffs, I don't finish until June, and I'm back on the ice in September."

"So you keep things casual."

"If that. I mean, I try to keep it so I'm a player on the ice, and only on the ice, know what I mean?"

And she respected him for it. "So this is just…"

"Two kisses. It's two kisses with a girl I knew a long time ago, who, to be honest, turns me on. But if you're wondering if I'm looking for a life partner in all of this, I'm not."

There was a finality to his voice that was unmistakeable. She wondered where that came from, and if the intensely private Cam Collier was hiding a broken heart somewhere.

"And if you don't want me to kiss you anymore, we

should probably stop running into each other. Because I like kissing you. A lot."

How she was still running and keeping her breath even was a mystery.

"It hasn't exactly been a hardship," she admitted. "Even if you won't speak at the benefit."

"Ouch. Nice dig, though, to deflect from your feelings about it."

"Hey, I didn't come here for a callout."

He laughed. They'd gone around the golf course and were heading back toward town. Normally, Hannah went over the Kissing Bridge and then along the Green, but she was wondering if that was a good idea today. They would not stop, that's for sure. The legend of the Kissing Bridge—that those who kissed on it would love forever—was just that, a legend. But she wasn't going to tempt fate in any way.

"I'm not looking for anything big, either," she admitted, though that wasn't exactly true. She'd admit to herself and no one else that she was lonely. That she sometimes longed for someone to share the evenings with, the breakfast table...maybe even babies. Just thinking about it made her heart hurt a little. But not Cam. Clearly, he was not a candidate for *that*.

They crossed the bridge and went down the Green, then worked their way back to where Hannah would normally climb the hill on her street and go home to get ready for work.

As they neared the stop sign, Cam kept pace with her and said, "Thanks for the run. It felt good to get out. And for clearing the air."

She looked over, and he was grinning that foolish grin again. Half the time she wanted to wipe it off his face, and the other half she wanted to burst out laughing. He was incorrigible.

"So long as we're clear," she replied, turning the corner and leaving him behind.

He said nothing, just kept on the road heading toward his parents' house. She halted and turned, watching him jog away. His butt was so very firm, his legs strong, and he'd hardly broken a sweat during their run. She'd be a bald-faced liar if she said his physicality wasn't a huge turn on. But it was more than that. It was his easygoing manner. The only time he'd been difficult was when she'd broached the idea of him reading for the benefit, but other than that, he was as chill as anyone she'd ever met.

She wondered how he'd accomplished that, since it was in such contrast to his ambition and drive. Cait and Claire were always saying that Hannah had no chill.

Her breath evened out as she walked up the hill to her house and decided that Cam's temperament was going to be one of life's mysteries she would probably never solve. And that was okay. He'd be gone after New Year's anyway.

CAM TOOK A DEEP BREATH AND PREPARED HIMSELF FOR A Friday evening at the rink. Connor was playing tonight, and the Gallaghers were big on showing up to cheer him on. Rory and Oaklee were going, and Cam couldn't say no to a kid who was super excited to be playing hockey. So he parked the SUV and made his way inside, looking for the Gallagher cheering section. They weren't hard to find. All he had to do was look for the red hair. The twins were more strawberry blond, Ethan and Aiden kept theirs cropped short, and the strands were more rusty than red. Rory had the lone dark head, like his mother, and Hannah's was a glorious mane of bright auburn, trailing over her shoulders.

Damn. They'd run together a few times this week, but her hair had always been up under her hat. He loved it down. Wanted to sink his hands into it.

Wanted to do a lot of things, actually.

All week, their interactions had been frustratingly platonic. A few runs around town. One stop at her office to give her the sponsorship money for the benefit. Crossing paths at the Ladybug Garden center, when he went to buy a huge poinsettia for his mom and Hannah was buying a wreath from one of Laurel's employees, George, who made them by hand.

He couldn't stop thinking about her. And while the runs had helped him burn off some energy, there was a lot more bundled up inside him, pounding to get out.

Oaklee waved him over, and he nodded at several people as he made his way through the stands. He was used to the stares and had expected them tonight. He'd say hello to people he hadn't seen in a while, probably sign a few autographs, and get nostalgic about how he'd been on that same ice twenty-five years earlier, with his first hockey stick.

He joined the group and smiled widely, feeling

instantly at home, as he always did with the Gallaghers. He shook John's hand and gave Moira a hug. They'd served as second parents to him during his childhood. Oaklee patted the bench beside her and Rory, and he sat down, resting his elbows on his knees. Down on the ice, around thirty seven-year-olds skated, wearing helmets and gloves and carrying sticks during the game warm-up. Connor's little brother, Ronan, sat with Grampa John, while Willow had baby Brenna on her lap. Aiden had Mandy in his arms, the baby bundled in a cute sweater and hat, while Laurel sat with yarn and needles, either knitting or crocheting something—Cam wasn't sure. Apparently, the twins had gone on a coffee run, which just left Hannah as the odd person out. She sat on the bench below him, and he reached out and tweaked a hank of her hair.

"Hello, Peeta." She turned around and gave him a bright smile, though her eyes showed she was surprised he'd done such a thing.

"Peeta?" he responded, leaning forward.

"P-I-T-A," she answered. "Like the bread. Stands for pain in the—"

"Right." He smirked. "Got your attention, though."

"If you're flirting, you need to work on your skills. Or maybe you save your mighty skills for the ice."

Beside him, Oaklee snorted.

"Maybe I like pestering you."

Rory joined in. "You sure loved bugging her when we were kids. Remember the time you asked her if she kept spare tampons in her purse?" Rory was already laughing when he added, "I swear, Hannah, I've never seen you blush like that in my life."

Cam did remember. Hannah was being a stuck-up senior while he and Rory were freshmen. She'd acted as if they were pesky little ants, always in her way and doing dumb things. Which, to be fair, they were—the current anecdote was a prime example. But her holier-than-thou attitude had always inspired Cam to be particularly impish. He'd loved getting under her skin.

"You guys were gross pimple-faced brats," she countered.

"Hey." Cam shook a finger at her. "I'll have you know I had excellent skin."

Oaklee responded now. "Oh, sure, Cam. The problem with you and Rory was that you two were very pretty, and you knew it." She rolled her eyes and Hannah laughed.

The kids went off the ice, the ref came out, and then both teams lined up at center ice for the face-off. There was a brief cheer, and then Hannah turned around again, looking up at Cam.

"We reordered all our signage and were able to put a rush on everything, so thanks," she said, her voice lower than it had been a moment ago.

"Glad I could help." He frowned. "Still no luck finding an author?"

She shook her head. "It's the weekend before Christmas. People have plans. No one wants to travel then. We got our first author because her family is nearby, and it worked out that she could go home for Christmas. That kind of magic doesn't happen twice."

Except he was here. And refused to help. He did feel guilty about it, whether she realized it or not. A few times, he'd almost reconsidered but then rejected the idea.

"It's only what, two weeks away?"

"Two weeks from tomorrow, yeah."

He nodded slowly. Then Hannah stood and said, "Scooch over. Trying to talk to you this way is killing my neck."

He shifted a little closer to Oaklee and made room between himself and Ethan. She settled in beside him, bringing the scent of vanilla and something floral with her. He didn't know if it was perfume or perhaps just her hair. Whatever it was, she smelled wonderful.

"Did you get the stuff I had couriered? It should have arrived today."

She shook her head. "It might take an extra day, being the holidays and all."

"I'll double check the tracking. It should be a nice addition to your auction, Hannah."

"Thanks." Once more, the unspoken thing was there between them. He was doing well, feeling good. He was here tonight, supporting Connor. So why was he so set on not participating in a more public way? He heard the questions in her mind without her needing to put voice to them.

For the first time in forever, he wondered if he should just say it. He could trust Hannah, couldn't he? What would happen if he straight up told her why he had said no? He glanced away from the ice and ten hurtling children and took in her profile. Hannah was a good person. Yeah, he and Rory had enjoyed annoying the crap out of her as kids. But he liked her, a lot. And she wasn't some stranger. She was the kind of woman— the kind of friend—who would keep a secret.

He mulled it over while watching the game, clapping and giving a shout of encouragement as Connor's team scored. The twins had come back with coffee, and the scent of the brew filled the air around them. At the end of the first period, a handful of locals ventured over to say hello and ask for autographs. For the first time in three weeks, Cam actually felt like himself. No lingering threat of a headache or fatigue. He hadn't had dizziness for days. Maybe this concussion wasn't as bad as everyone had thought. He had an appointment next week for another evaluation. Maybe he could even be back practicing on the ice before Christmas. He could always fly back for the holiday so he'd be with his family, as promised.

When the second period started, everyone took their seats in the stands again. Hannah had shifted to his other side and was talking to Oaklee, not about the benefit, but about the last chamber of commerce meeting and something about profit percentages and local retail traffic for the Christmas season, and how it was down slightly over last year. As he eavesdropped, he suddenly realized what it was about Hannah that intimi- dated him. It wasn't her looks, though she was—and always had been—stunning. It wasn't that she was older than he was. Or that she had a reputation of being a bit of a ballbuster. He could handle all those things. He liked a challenge, after all.

No, it was her brain. Hannah had always been the smartest person he knew. If she'd wanted, she could have gone on to be a CEO of a major corporation, and done it with ease. Clearly, she liked what she did, enjoyed running her own business, loved real estate. Rory said that she was involved in a few other ventures as well, as an investor.

Hannah was everything he wasn't. He struggled to read. He could do math, but even that had been a challenge as he'd had difficulty reading the questions. He'd had a tutor once he left school to play full time, and he'd been pushed through academically because he was a prodigy on ice.

But he couldn't compete with Hannah Gallagher in the brains department.

And it would be painfully obvious if he went ahead and told her his reasons for not speaking at her event.

No matter what he did, he would disappoint her.

He focused on the game, watching the kids, watching Connor in particular. He was a strong skater, fast for his age, and pretty steady. He had good ice awareness, too, but the stick looked awkward in his hands, and he struggled to control the puck. Granted, he was only seven, but Cam thought it might be fun to take him out on an outdoor pond and give him some tips. He'd mention it to Ethan and Willow later.

The other team scored, and the crowd on the other side of the ice stomped their feet and hollered. As the teams lined up for the face-off, Hannah's leg brushed against his. He looked over at her and found her watching him, the gleam in her eyes telegraphing something he hoped he was interpreting correctly.

They'd been doing this dance for well over a week. And maybe he wasn't the mental giant she was, but he could hold his own when it came to the bedroom. His physicality had always been his best asset. This was far more in his comfort zone.

He slid his hand down and grazed a finger over her jean-clad knee. She was wearing tight skinnies that were tucked into those brown boots she liked so much. She gasped slightly at the covert touch, and his lips curved in silent gratification. He grazed the outside of her thigh for long seconds, a tacit reminder this was not an accidental touch. But he didn't look at her. He didn't need to. He could feel the tension in her thigh muscles, and anticipation settled low in his pelvis.

Hannah was in fantastic shape, strong and lean. He imagined her body curled around his and let out a deep breath, pulling his hand away from her leg. If he wasn't careful, he was going to be sitting here with a hard-on for the rest of the game.

They didn't talk after that, and after the game was over, Willow invited everyone back to The Purple Pig for hot chocolate and cookies. Hannah was going, and the invitation was extended to Cam as well. He was going to offer to drive her over, but she joined Laurel and Willow, who were walking with the babies. Instead, Ethan invited him to visit the team in the locker room, and Cam readily agreed. He loved this kind of thing. One of his favourite days of the year was the open team practice on March break, when the local youth got to interact with the players.

Connor was instantly a celebrity as he introduced his Uncle Rory's friend, Cam. Cam chatted to the team, offering tons of praise and a few hints to up their game, and then he and Ethan, who was holding Ronan's hand, collected Connor and his duffel and headed out of the rink.

"You want to drive with me, buddy?" he asked Connor.

"Seriously?"

He chuckled. "Sure. Throw your hockey bag in your dad's truck, though. P-U."

Connor laughed and raced off to Ethan's truck, then he trotted back and hopped up in the seat next to Cam. "Hey, thanks for coming to the locker room. The guys were like so excited!"

"No problem, buddy. You did a good job out there. You're a good skater."

"I am?"

"Sure are. You want to do some stick work sometime? I kinda miss being on the ice."

Connor looked at him with eyes as large as saucers. "Um, duh," he replied. "My dad made us an outdoor rink this year. It's kinda small, though."

"It's big enough. I'll talk to your dad, okay?"

"Okay. Thanks, uh…"

"Just call me Cam, Connor."

Connor grinned so big that Cam could see the two teeth he had missing. Damn, he was a cute kid.

But when they got to The Purple Pig and walked

inside, Connor disappeared and Cam's gaze homed in on Hannah, laughing at something Laurel was saying as the two of them carried cookies to the tables that had been pushed together to seat the entire family.

Hannah. The night wasn't over for them. If he had his way, it was just beginning.

6

Hannah had never been so aware of a man in her entire life.

Sitting beside Cam at the rink had been an interesting experience. First of all, it was clear as the nose on his face that the building was his home, whether he was on or off the ice. His body language had been more relaxed than she'd seen since his arrival, his smile ready and genuine. It was his comfort zone, and that casual confidence only made him more attractive to her. There was something about a confident man that turned her crank, and while Cam had always had a certain low-key arrogance about him, tonight she realized it was most powerful when he was able to simply be himself.

It was something she envied.

He'd taken the time to sign autographs, again, and then gone into the locker room with Connor's team. It was all Connor could talk about now, and Cam just smiled and laughed along as if it was no big deal. As if he were no big deal.

But to her, he was a big deal. His refusal to appear at the event was still something that puzzled her, because every other thing she was learning about Cam Collier was that he was a really nice guy with, as he put it, a smokin' hot bod, and a career so spectacular that he was one of the few men who didn't find her threatening. If anything, he'd gone on to definitely out-achieve the achiever.

Of course, they wouldn't have a relationship. But it had been months—years—since she'd been involved with a man, and for Pete's sake, it was Christmas. If he was interested, why not? He'd go back to Denver, and they'd chalk it up to that one Christmas they had a fling. Not that anyone had to know.

And if it was out of character for her, so what? She was thirty-three years old. She could do something crazy if she damned well wanted.

It was eight thirty before the cookies were gone and the mugs emptied. Ethan made noises about getting the boys home for bed, and the babies were already asleep in their mothers' arms. Hannah and Oaklee got up and cleared the mess, loading the dishes in commercial dishwasher as Emily, the café manager, finished closing procedures. When Hannah came out of the kitchen again, Cam was moving the tables to their original position and tucking the chairs in properly. Damn, he fit in so well. He always had. Rory snagged a chair, and the two of them shared a laugh. Maybe this was a mistake. Maybe a fling should be with someone with no ties to the family at all. It had so much potential to be awkward.

But someone else wouldn't be Cam. Wouldn't be tall like Cam, wouldn't have the same hair, or the full lips, or the hard, muscled thighs she'd gotten a glimpse of during their runs. No, she wanted him. And the way he'd touched her in the stands tonight told her he wanted her, too.

They all left through the front door, Emily locking behind them, and Cam appeared at her shoulder.

"I'll drive you home," he said, his voice low. It wasn't a suggestion. It was an invitation and an acceptance all in one, and her body responded to the low timbre of his voice by breaking out in goose bumps.

"I guess that would be okay," she answered easily, hoping the rest of the family didn't pick up on their edgy energy.

The interior of his SUV enclosed them in a cocoon of intimacy. He cranked up the heater as the temperature had dropped, and silence filled the space as he pulled away from the curb and headed down Main to the turnoff to her street. Had she ever been this aware of a man before? Had she ever wanted one quite this much? It had all changed tonight, with the nudge of her knee against his, meeting his gaze, and seeing acknowledgment in his eyes.

Her pelvic muscles tightened. Oh, this was going to be so good.

It took maybe two minutes to get from the café to her house. She looked up at it, gleaming in the December darkness. She'd turned on the lights before leaving tonight, and the eaves, front railing, and shrubs twinkled with clear lights. The railing lights illuminated the wreath on the front door, and a warmth filled her heart at the sight. She loved this little house. It wasn't as big and fancy as some, which had surprised her family. Instead, it was cozy and welcoming. Of course, she'd gutted a lot of the interior and made it her own. Maybe she was going through this world solo instead of half of a pair, but this was *home*.

And Cam was going to be inside it. She'd never brought a man here before, and she tried not to read too much into that fact.

He unclipped his seatbelt, the click unusually loud in the darkness. Her breath caught in her chest as he got out and went around the hood to open her door.

She stepped out and looked up at him. For a moment, she wondered if he was going to press her against the door with his hard, strong body and kiss her. The hungry look in his eyes certainly telegraphed that he wanted to. But instead, he held out his hand, and she took it, hoping he couldn't tell how much she was shaking. This wasn't like her. She was the kind of woman who doled out great advice but rarely took it herself. Who teased her friends about getting laid but went home alone. Who advised those she loved to relax, but scheduled her own life to the hour.

Nothing about this thing with Cam was scheduled. Not even a little bit.

He waited while she unlocked the door, and they stepped inside.

She'd turned the outside lights on but not inside. The house was dark, lit only slightly by the tangential glow from the mini-bulbs on the porch and in the evergreens. She took off her coat. He took off his, too, and hung them both on the carved hooks in the foyer. She unzipped her boots and toed them off; he removed his shoes and left them on the mat. Neither of them had said a single word since leaving The Purple Pig. And before she could think of what she could possibly say now, his arms came around her, his hands gripped her butt, and he lifted her up until her legs instinctively wrapped around him.

Then he kissed her.

It wasn't wild and uncontrolled. It was a full-on, deliberate meltdown of her senses as his mouth possessed hers. He took four strong steps, and she found her back pressed against the support wall between the kitchen and hall. Cam pinned her there with his body, and she held on, gasping as his mouth slid away from hers and instead raced down her neck. If she could have tilted her head back, she would have, but it was pressed against the unrelenting wall as he slid his tongue into the hollow of her throat, sending shivers of delight rippling through her body.

"Cam," she finally said, the sound strangled with desire.

He still didn't say anything, and for some reason, she found it incredibly arousing. Instead, he tilted his hips, keeping her in place while his fingers got busy with the buttons on her shirt.

The soft brushed cotton slipped open, and he reached behind her and flicked open the clasp of her bra. Her breasts weren't overly large. On a generous day, she'd call them a C cup, but the sound of approval from

Cam's throat made her feel as if they were the most amazing things in the world. She was a tangle of shirt and bra, with a bra cup riding up toward her neck, but she didn't give a damn as he fastened his mouth on one very ready nipple.

She cried out, and her hips jerked against him. He was in total control, and she was rapidly becoming a boneless, desperate mush. "Too many clothes." Her voice was strident in the silence. "Let me down, Cam."

He didn't acquiesce for a few moments as he feasted on the other breast, his hot mouth undoing her bit by bit. But she pressed against him again, and he braced his hands on her bottom and let her body slide down the wall.

Once she was free, she found the strength to meet him equally. She pulled off her shirt and bra and left them on the floor, then reached for his sweater and pulled it over his head so that his torso was delightfully naked. Oh, glory. Muscles curved and dipped everywhere, shoulders and arms and pecs and a delicious six pack before everything dipped low into the waistband of his jeans. His eyes were dark fire as he met her gaze and then reached for the button of her jeans. She reached for his at the same time, and somehow they stumbled out of them in the hallway, until she was only wearing bikini panties and he was in boxer briefs that hugged his ass and thighs like a dream. It hugged something else, too, and once again her muscles tightened in anticipation.

He reached for his jeans, pulled something out of the pocket, and then reached for her. They were in the hallway now, and she knew she should lead him to her bedroom, but he caught her in his arms and managed to slide his hand inside her panties. She cried out again, overwhelmed by the sensations racing through her, but not so overwhelmed she couldn't meet him halfway. Her hand molded to the ridge in his briefs, and he groaned as he kissed her, the sound vibrating from her mouth throughout her whole body.

She pushed down his briefs and took him in her hand, her grip firm and purposeful. In response, he got her panties down to her knees, and for a few frantic moments, they pleasured each other with their hands.

"Cam...I can't stand up any longer. You've got to take me to bed, Cam."

He pushed her panties the rest of the way down, and his underwear, too, and once against picked her up so she was straddling him. "Which door?"

"The last one on the left."

He was walking, and she was sucking on his neck, and within two seconds, he was in her bedroom and kicking the door shut with his foot. Then, instead of putting her down, he pinned her against the door. "Hang on," he ordered, and she tightened her legs around him. She heard a tear and felt his hands move, then realized he'd put on a condom.

She wished he'd hurry.

They never made it to the bed. He adjusted her, then slid inside her, right against the door to her bedroom. It was elemental, beautifully physical, and she gave herself over to the sensation of him filling her again...and again...and again. At one point, he reached down between them, and she called out with pleasure as spasms rocked her body. Moments later, he thrust so hard she wondered if they'd break the door.

And then he stilled, his breaths coming fast, her body limp, her brain empty.

Only then did he carry her to the bed and let her down gently on the comforter before collapsing beside her.

Cam needed a minute to catch his breath and feel his body again.

He hadn't expected her to be so primal, so responsive to his every touch. Maybe he should have anticipated her response. After all, Hannah never did anything halfway. And he hadn't been wrong. Her body was a pure delight, all small curves and tight muscle and breasts that were the perfect size, round and firm and yet soft, too. They'd driven him crazy from the moment he'd unsnapped her bra.

For God's sake, they'd left a trail of clothing from her foyer to the bedroom. He'd expected there to be some urgency. He hadn't expected it would be incendiary.

"Hey, Han? Bathroom?"

A low chuckle sounded beside him. "First door is the closet. Second is the en suite."

He got up from the bed and went to take care of the condom. When he returned, she was still sprawled on the bed, naked as the day she was born, and holy hell, she was beautiful. His eyes had adjusted to the dark, and he could see her burnished hair spread out on her pillow, the hollows of her hips, the tips of her breasts. He'd brought one condom. One. It was the only regret he had of the evening.

And now he was standing naked at the foot of her bed.

She started to laugh, a soft chuckle that made him smile in response. "What?"

"You look good naked."

"So do you, Hannah Banana."

She raised up on her elbows. "Come here," she said, "and catch your breath."

He went back to the bed and lay down beside her, turned onto his side so he was facing her profile. How could it be that he wanted her again so soon? Why had he thought one condom would be enough?

Hannah was demanding. He should have known better.

"Sorry it was so rushed," he said, bracing his elbow and resting his head on his hand. It hadn't even been fifteen minutes since he'd parked at the curb.

"It was perfect." She sighed, leaning her head back. She was still braced on her elbows, so the movement made her breasts jut forward.

He couldn't dispute it. He hadn't been with a woman for a long time, but this…this was one for the books.

Maybe because for the first time, he hadn't been with someone who saw him as Cam the Superstar. He was Cam, the pain-in-the-ass friend of her little brother.

And if he'd rocked her world, she'd destroyed his—in the best possible way.

"Do you have to go right away?" she asked, finally dropping down from her elbows and shifting to her side beside him.

He laughed. "I'm a big boy. I don't have a curfew."

"Except people will see your SUV. And you're staying with your parents."

"Well, well. You're worried about what people will think."

She met his gaze in the dim light. Somewhere down the street, there was a dusk-to-dawn lamp, and it gave enough light to show her features in black and white. He reached out and grazed her hip with his fingers, then the hollow of her waist.

"Actually," she said, "I don't care. People can mind their own business. Or talk. I just keep doing my thing."

"Which is something I've always liked about you."

"Thanks."

They were quiet for a few moments. Then Cam felt the need to come clean about what he figured were expectations.

"I've been symptom free for several days now. I'm going to see if I can practice with the team after my next follow-up appointment."

"You must be happy about that."

"I am. But even if I practice, I don't think I'll be in the lineup until after New Year's. I still plan to spend Christmas with my family." He took a breath and held it for a moment. "And with you." There was a hesitant moment after he said the words, where he nearly added, "if that's okay."

She touched his hand where it rested on her hip. "Listen, we both know what this is and isn't. Your life is there. Mine is here. Right now, we're insanely attracted to each other. That's all this is, Cam. You don't have to worry about me getting over attached."

He should feel relief, but instead, unease settled through him. Was he really so forgettable?

Then he gave himself a mental shake. That wasn't what she was saying at all. She was just being realistic about their situation, saving him from having to say it, that was all.

She reached out and touched him, soft, fluttery touches that he revelled in. "You feel so good," she whispered. "You have a six pack. I can feel the ridges with my fingertips. Is it wrong that your body turns me on so much?"

"If it is, I'm equally guilty," he confessed. His hand slid from her hip to the soft spot on her inner thigh. "Hannah, I only brought one condom."

"Well, shit."

He laughed out loud then. He liked her so damned much. She was smart, funny, hot. There actually wasn't anything about Hannah he didn't like.

"Don't worry," he murmured, sliding closer, slipping his hand between her thighs. "I have a few ideas."

"More than one way to score, Collier?"

"Mmm." He leaned forward and nuzzled at her breasts.

Her hands slid into his hair. "It doesn't always take a

slap shot, right? I mean, you could come up on the wing and catch a rebound—"

"We could swap hockey jokes all night," he replied, kissing his way toward her navel as her breath released on a hiss. "But my mouth is gonna be a little bit busy."

And it was.

7

He ended up staying the night.

Hannah woke at seven, a full hour later than normal, and stretched, her muscles flexing and releasing beneath the soft sheets. Cam was beside her, his hair flat on one side, and his long lashes resting on the crests of his cheeks. At some point, he'd gone to the hallway and retrieved his shorts. Hannah had been too lazy. She was still completely naked.

Cam Collier. Go figure.

Her cheeks heated as she remembered last night. Maybe they'd only had one condom, but they'd been inventive. A few times, actually. Hannah was used to being in control, but she'd been in total surrender mode with Cam. Surrender not only to him, but to her desires, surprising not only him, but herself as well. The word wanton came to mind. And Cam… He'd been amazing. Everything.

She let out a slow, quiet breath. Okay, so they were

sexually compatible. That's all this was. Letting loose, blowing off steam, enjoying each other.

Except she looked at his slumbering face and felt a tenderness wash over her.

It was just because she'd known him so long. He was her little brother's best friend, after all. Heck, she could still remember when Cam's voice had started to change.

She slipped out of bed and went to the bathroom, turning on the shower before grabbing a fresh towel from the shelf. She made it quick, then bundled her hair in the towel and grabbed a second to wrap around her body. Her clothes were all in the bedroom, so taking a deep breath, she stepped outside the steamy bathroom and into the cooler air of her room.

Cam was sitting up in bed, his eyes closed, tension lines around his eyes and his lips.

She hurried to the edge of the bed and perched on the mattress. "What is it?" she asked.

"Headache," he murmured. He opened his eyes and she saw pain there. "Shit."

She kept her voice low as her heart sank. He'd been feeling so good. "Do you feel sick to your stomach?"

"A little woozy, yeah."

"What can you take for pain?"

"What have you got?"

"Acetaminophen and naproxen."

"Naproxen. Acetaminophen doesn't do jack."

She grabbed her robe from the back of the door and wrapped it around herself, dropping the towel. Then she went to the kitchen for the medication, water, and an ice pack. When she returned, she watched as he took the pills and then put the ice pack on the back of his neck. "Here. Keep this here for a few minutes and see if it helps." As he held it, she went to the bathroom and got a ginger tablet. "Take this, too," she said, handing it over. "It'll help settle your stomach." She sat on the edge of the bed again. "Any double vision, blurred vision, that kind of thing?"

He shook his head a little. "No. Just the sick headache."

"I'm sorry, Cam. I know this means you have to restart the clock on being symptom free."

He nodded.

A smile flirted with the corners of her mouth. "I guess we overdid it last night."

He took the ice pack from the back of his neck and looked at her. "Totally worth it," he answered, and her insides curled with both memory and anticipation.

It was Saturday, so Hannah didn't have to go into the office. Truthfully, she had been planning to work on the silent-auction items today, as well as firm up other details with participating businesses. She and Oaklee were meeting later to discuss dinner-ticket sales, which had slowed since the announcement of the loss of their headliner.

But right now, there was nowhere she needed to be.

"Lie down and close your eyes while the meds kick in. I'll go make some breakfast."

"I should probably go. My car—"

"Your car's been out front all night. Another few hours won't matter, and honestly…who cares?" Darling was small. People were going to talk anyway. Hannah tried not to listen to it. Or at the very least, not repeat it. "I'm thirty-three, Cam. I'm a big girl who can live her own life."

He chuckled. "Lucky you."

Her smiled slid off her face. "Oh wait. I never thought that maybe you would like to keep this off the radar. I know you like to keep your private life private."

Cam shrugged and met her gaze. "I don't care about the public, to be honest. Not right now. It's more... I don't want to get sucker punched by Rory for hooking up with his sister. Or, you know, look your mom in the eye and see...you know."

Aw, that was sweet. He didn't want to disappoint her family. She liked that about him. In fact, she was discovering there wasn't a whole lot she didn't like.

"Then it's up to you. If you need me to, I can drive your rental to your folks' place if you think you shouldn't be driving. Or you're welcome to stay. I'm not about to kick you out after a night of debauchery." She wiggled her eyebrows, and he laughed again.

"I'll stay for a while. You mentioned food. It's always a good incentive."

"Now I see you were only after my cooking."

He reached out and slid his hand up the outside of her thigh, underneath the robe. "Not just your cooking. But I'm not sure another round would be good for my head."

She bit down on her lip and got up from the edge of the bed. "Right. Then breakfast it is."

Hannah hurried to the kitchen and once there, tightened the belt on her robe.

She'd make him eggs and avocado toast, and then by that time, she might have figured out where she wanted this to go next.

Cam knew he should put on his clothes and head home. Or go hang out somewhere. Be anywhere but playing house with Hannah Gallagher, but he was sitting in her sunny kitchen for two reasons. One, she'd just fed him an amazing breakfast and poured him a second cup of coffee. And two, his head was still in a fragile state. The pain was mostly gone, thanks to medicine and an extra thirty minutes of quiet in bed while she cooked. But now he had a headache hangover, like it could rebound at any moment.

He was going to take his time. Besides, being with Hannah wasn't exactly a hardship. Her house was lovely, cozy, and welcoming, with splashes of panache that were very her. The sofa he was sitting on was plush and comfortable, but both the throw rug in the middle of the floor and the art above the fireplace mantle were abstract, with splashes of rusty orange in with tan and sage green. The rust color reminded him of her hair, and he sat back and sipped the rich coffee while remembering how her hair had grazed his thighs last night…

The thought was erased from his brain as she entered the room carrying her laptop and a binder in her hands and with glasses perched on her nose. Damned if she didn't look adorable and fiercely smart all wrapped up in one package.

"Whatcha got there?" he asked, angling himself a little and tucking one leg beneath him.

"Stuff about the benefit. I'm going to inventory our silent-auction items today, and later, Oaklee is going to come over, and we're going to go over our ticket sales for the dinner." She frowned. "Last year at this time, we were within ten seats of being sold out."

"And this year you're not?"

She shook her head. "And the price hasn't gone up. The golf club is doing it for the same as last year. The only thing I can think of is that we've cancelled our speaker and are just doing the auction."

"Maybe what you need is something to really bring them in to bid."

She reached into her binder for a sheaf of papers and handed them over. "Well, if you have any suggestions…this is what we have."

He took the papers and scanned them. If he slowed down and really focused, he would be able to make sense of them. A few words he recognized stood out, like the Foxborough Inn, and something yoga. "See?" she asked. "We've got some great things lined up already."

"I, uh, see," he agreed.

"What do you think of this one?" She leaned over and pointed to an item. Any other time, Cam would be able to suss it out by taking his time, but right now, he was flustered and couldn't focus. "Um, Han, things are a little blurred," he lied. Something heavy settled in the pit of his stomach. He was using his freaking injury to cover his disability. What a coward he was. Why couldn't he just tell her?

Because last night, she'd looked at him like he was a freaking god, and he wasn't sure he could bear falling from that pedestal. Everyone seemed to think he was this invincible wonder kid. Instead, he was a fraud. And now, Hannah was looking at him with worry wrinkling her brow and clouding her eyes.

"You didn't say that earlier. Do you need to call a doctor or something?"

He felt even more of a heel for making her worry. "No, I'm sure it's fine. I just need to take it easy. It's just the fine print stuff kind of blurring together, that's all."

Hannah took the sheets back. "Let me drive you home, though. You shouldn't be behind the wheel if your vision is compromised." She leaned forward and peered into his eyes. "And if things get worse, you should call your doctor."

They wouldn't get worse. His vision was fine, and his headache was nearly gone. But he couldn't tell her that. He'd let her think he was sick before admitting a weakness, wouldn't he?

Coward. You could make this thing a success for her if you'd just own up.

Instead, he put his hand on her knee. "What you need isn't something that everyone can bid on, but a draw that only attendees can enter." He grinned. "Like two tickets to a Stanley Cup final game, along with travel and hotel for two nights."

She stared at him.

He shrugged. "I can make that happen. Oaklee can promote the hell out of it on social media and radio."

Her eyes filled with tears. "You'd do that?"

"It's only money, Hannah. What else am I going to do with it?"

It was the right thing to offer. Hannah ran with the idea and within an hour had sent it to Oaklee so she could start designing a graphic.

He was happy to help. He really was. But there was a part of him, inside, that wished he could put that happy expression on her face without having to buy its way there.

8

Hannah got busier as the day of the benefit drew closer. Two house sales closed, and she saw her clients through getting their keys and stepping foot in their new homes. Showings dropped off a bit in the lead up to the holiday, as most people were in Christmas mode and rushing around to do their shopping and decorating. But Hannah hadn't yet put up her tree, nor had she wrapped the presents she'd bought for family. And the day-long event was taking a significant amount of her time. Christmas was a busy time for Oaklee, too, as the town held several events and promotions, and as social media manager, Oaklee was scheduled to the hilt. Hannah didn't feel she could add anything more to Oaklee's plate.

But she still made time for her morning run, though the last few days she'd been running solo. Right now, she was back to her original route, her feet slapping the sidewalk in a steady rhythm as her breath made puffs of air around her face. Her early runs were the one thing that always seemed to keep her sane. Whether it was the endorphins or the deep breathing or what, exercise kept Hannah from being overwhelmed.

She missed running with Cam, though. She hadn't talked to him since she'd driven him home, and she suspected he was skipping the runs due to his recurring symptoms.

She'd wanted to call him or text him, but maybe the one night was all he was after, and truthfully, she wasn't sure more was a good idea. She was in danger of liking him too much. For the first time in a long time, she felt as if she could be herself with someone. Cam had no reason to feel threatened by her "big personality," as her brother, Ethan, put it. The morning after he'd stayed the night, they'd talked a long time about why she loved real estate, why she found business so invigorating, and she'd even let him in on the secret that she was a silent partner in a few ventures around town, Willow's yoga studio included. He'd shared with her, too, about what it was like to be a professional athlete, the pressure, the competitiveness, the fame. They were a pair of overachievers who didn't have to compete with each other. It was just too bad they lived on opposite sides of the country. Maybe they might have explored this thing between them a little further. See where it led.

When she got home, there was a text on her phone from him, asking her to meet him for lunch at the Sugarbush Diner. She knew she should say no. What was the point in prolonging something that had a definite shelf life? And yet she found herself typing back yes for twelve thirty. She wanted to see him. To know how he was doing, and if he was feeling better.

Besides, the diner had the best Cobb salad in Vermont. She'd been indulging in a little too much comfort food lately. She could use fewer starchy carbs and more protein right now.

Hannah walked in at twelve twenty, a few minutes early, and to her surprise he was already in a booth, his menu closed in front of him and a large glass of ice water at his elbow. She slid into the booth and smiled. "Hey. It's good to see you."

His face lit up, and it did silly things to her insides. "You, too," he said. Then he laughed. "This place hasn't changed a bit. Neither the menu nor the Christmas decorations."

There was an artificial tree toward the back, and all sorts of garish tinsel decorating the booths and beams. Each table had a small artificial poinsettia in the middle. "It's delightfully cheesy," Hannah agreed. "And it wouldn't be Christmas at the Sugarbush without all of it."

A waitress came over and took Hannah's order for water, and then Hannah asked for the salad, and Cam ordered a club sandwich with salad instead of fries. "Trying to behave yourself?" she asked, handing over the plastic menus.

He nodded to the waitress and then shrugged in Hannah's direction. "I'm not training, and Mom is determined to make home-cooked meals every day. It's not going to be good if I get too soft while I'm home."

"You're going to miss out on the maple crème pie

then," she replied, putting on a sad face. "It's something." Then she held his gaze. "How are you feeling?"

"I saw the doctor. I'm fine. Just a setback, but that morning was the exception. I've been fine since."

"So…"

"So you broke me, Hannah Banana."

There was a gleam in his eye that made her blush. "Shut up," she murmured, wishing the waitress would come back with her water.

"No, seriously. The doc said I probably overdid it. Set me back a little." He leaned forward. "But just so you know, it was totally worth it."

"Cam." Her voice was a low warning. The waitress came back with her water and a refill for Cam, along with a shy smile for the celebrity. Hannah rolled her eyes.

Cam took a sip, and so did Hannah, and then he leaned forward again. "So I bet you've spent the last few days itemizing all the reasons why us not seeing each other again is a good thing."

Busted. "Oh, you think you're so smart."

"I've known you a long time. The thing is, when we really want something, we can always come up with reasons to logically justify our behavior. So for example, I might say that we both know this is a short-term thing, so why not enjoy it?"

She swallowed against a growing lump in her throat and reached down to fiddle with her napkin. Yeah, she'd used that argument before. Including the night they'd gone back to her place.

"Or maybe that this is good because we know each

other and there won't be any expectations for more than
either of us can give."

"Cam—"

"Because we kind of trust each other."

"Really, keep your voice down—"

"And we *really* like being together."

She gave up. She stopped fingering the paper napkin
and let out a sigh. "You overdid it, remember? A repeat
is not a good idea."

"*Au contraire*." She laughed at the expression despite
herself. Cam ran his finger along the edge of his glass. "I
believe what the doctor said was to pace myself."

The lump was nearly impossible to swallow around
now. How could he be sitting there discussing this as
casually as they might discuss the weather forecast?
"Pace yourself."

"You know. Slow down. Not be in such a hurry. Take
my time."

The heat from her cheeks spread throughout her
body. "You're seducing me in broad daylight," she whispered, hoping no one could hear them. At least the
chatter from the other patrons and the Christmas music
playing on the speakers caused some auditory inter-
ference.

"Is it working?"

It so was, and she didn't want to admit it. She looked
up at him and brushed her hair back off her shoulder.
"What would be the point of us being together? I mean,
clearly there's chemistry. I'm not denying that. But
you're heading back to Denver. I'm going to be here.

And I really don't do relationships." She lifted her chin. "I'm too busy."

He studied her for a long moment. Long enough that she thought he might see through that last statement for what it was defense mechanism. She loved to work. Was there anything wrong with that? And working meant she didn't have time to think about the dearth of sex or intimacy in her life since Liam walked out.

Much, anyway.

"I don't, either. But I like being with you, Hannah. Sometimes it's good to feel, I don't know, alive. Like there's more to life than a puck on the ice and..."

He halted, sat back as the waitress brought their food. He thanked her and then picked up his fork, but he only pushed a piece of cucumber around with it.

"And what?" she asked.

He shrugged. "My body isn't going to let me do this forever. Eventually, there has to be something else. It's kind of scary, because since I was a kid, there has never *been* anything other than hockey. I have no idea what's next. And with this injury... I haven't been able to avoid thinking about it."

She thought about that. Then thought about her high school years, university, getting her Realtor's license, setting up her own business, her entrepreneurial streak.

"Cam, know what? We suck at a life/work balance."

He grinned and finally stabbed the cucumber. "That's kind of what I'm saying, Han. We've got a couple of weeks here where maybe we can be a little better at that. With each other."

"Our families will talk."

He rolled his eyes. "Whatever. We're adults, aren't we?"

"And so will the town."

"Probably. Probably about how Cam Collier is a lucky bastard. You, Ms. Gallagher, are notorious for having high standards. I'm flattered that I've made the cut."

They were actually talking about having a short-term but not-sneaking-around kind of relationship. What she really liked was how Cam seemed to see the very things she'd been criticized for by partners of the past as attributes and qualities.

"You want to go on a date, then?"

He nodded. "I do. A real date."

She got that tingly feeling again, and not because she was thinking of him kissing her or touching her, but that he was asking to spend actual time with her. Enjoying her company.

"What's your idea of a perfect date?" she asked, trying to settle her nerves. She drizzled dressing on her salad and forced herself to start eating.

"I'm a low-key kind of guy. A movie? Maybe ice cream, or a few drinks after." He grinned. "Chicken wings or nachos. A walk in the park. Something that makes you laugh."

Damn, he was good at throwing in those after-thoughts that hit her right in the feels. And she liked all those things, too. She also liked intimate dinners, the theater, and wouldn't be totally averse to a grand gesture or two. But it wasn't necessary. For all her peculiarities and perceived high standards, Hannah could be incredibly low-maintenance.

"What's yours?" he asked. "So I have a somewhere to start."

"You're going to plan a date?"

He frowned. "Well, yeah. But I only want a starting point. It might be fun to throw in a surprise or two."

He'd certainly surprised her last Friday night. If all his surprises were that good, she wasn't going to complain.

"Good wine, cozy fires, anything that makes me feel…special. Like the person I'm with thinks I'm…" Her voice stumbled a bit. "Worth the effort."

He'd been holding a triangle of sandwich, but he put it down and wiped his fingers, focusing all his attention on her. "Damn, Hannah. Any guy who doesn't think you're worth the effort is a fool. All right. Tell you what. Tomorrow night, I'm taking you on a date. I'll pick you up at seven." He frowned for a moment, then his face cleared. "Wear those boots that you like so much, and dress warmly."

Oh Lordy. What was he planning?

"Cam, you don't have to—

"Yes, I do." He picked up his sandwich again. "I might not be here for more than a few weeks, but I can damned well make sure you are treated the way you deserve." He bit into the sandwich, chewed, swallowed, and dabbed his mouth. "The way you've always deserved," he stated, reaching for his water. He took a sip, put the glass down, and pointed at her. "None of those clowns in school ever appreciated you. Including me."

She snorted, trying not to be touched and failing, but covering it with a laugh. "Dude, you were thirteen."

He grinned then, dazzling her with his smile. "Yeah, but I was an *old* thirteen," he replied.

It was so silly she couldn't help but laugh, then she dug into her salad again. It had been a long time since she'd been wooed. If she could only have it for a short time, she was going to enjoy it. And she'd deal with missing him when he was gone.

Because she was going to miss him. Funny how after all this time, everything had changed. They'd been in each other's orbits since they were kids, but in just a few weeks, they'd become so much closer. Not because of his long-standing friendship with Rory, but despite it.

They finished their lunch, and Cam walked her back to her office. They stopped at the door, and the scent of evergreen from the lush wreath filled Hannah's nostrils. She'd pulled on gloves and wrapped her scarf around her neck, and Cam's nose was red from the cold. But she was warm all over, just from being with him.

"Tomorrow. Seven, and I'll pick you up at your house."

"Seven," she parroted, and made the mistake of dropping her gaze to his lips.

Her eyes darted up again to meet his, realizing there were little flecks of green and gold in the dark depths. The tip of his tongue snuck out and ran along his lower lip, and her breath caught. She should go in. They were in the middle of busy Main Street. And yet she hesitated, long enough that he leaned forward a few inches and placed a soft, quick-but-lingering kiss on her lips.

"Tomorrow," he reminded her, and then turned away.

Her lips tingled, and she watched the pockets of his jeans as he walked away.

Cam Collier, hockey superstar, Darling's golden son, had spent the night in her bed and had just kissed her in the middle of the day on a busy street.

Christmas was a magical time indeed.

9

Cam couldn't remember the last time he'd been this nervous about a date.

He had everything he needed in the back of the SUV. He'd made phone calls today and set it all up the way he wanted. It was not necessarily elaborate or glamorous, but he'd listened to what Hannah had said yesterday, and he'd realized that her perfect date wasn't something crazy and expensive. Rather, she wanted—no, needed—someone to put thought and effort into it. So he'd enlisted the help of Willow for the food and Rory for information about who he needed to call for permissions. Right after Rory had delivered a speech about not hurting his sister that had ended with the words, "Don't be a douchebag."

Cam parked in front of her house and took a deep breath. Tonight wasn't just about a date. Tonight, he was going to tell her the real reason why he wouldn't speak at her event. It was something he'd never come right out and told anyone before. He'd never trusted anyone with it, not even Rory. But it was time. He couldn't run from it forever. Especially when thinking about the future and what he might do after retirement.

She came out of the house dressed warmly and wearing those sexy brown boots that stopped just shy of her kneecaps. The hem of her coat rested below her butt, and she had on mittens and a knit cap that sat sideways, like a beret. She was adorable, framed by the Christmas lights on her front porch. His heart gave a solid thump as she came down the steps and he hopped out to open her door.

"Hi," she said, a little breathless. She smelled delicious, like sugar cookies, and he wanted to taste her skin. Instead, he dropped a kiss on her cheek and reached for the door handle.

"You look great," he said, trying not to choke on his own spit, feeling like he was sixteen and borrowing his father's car to take out a girl.

"So do you," she replied, hopping up into the seat. "I like your ass in those jeans."

Heat rushed up his cheeks, though he had no idea why. She'd been up close and personal with his ass already, but tonight was different. It was…deliberate, and every word held new weight.

He jogged around the hood of the car, got in, and adjusted the heater. "Warm enough?"

"Perfect." She smiled by the light of the dashboard, and his heart thumped again.

Hannah. His brain jolted back by a week to the

night they'd spent in her bed. There'd been less thinking then, and more acting on a need, a desire that had been awakened. It had blown his mind, but there was more now. There were feelings involved, tender ones. Cam wasn't sure what to do with that. He'd never been the tender-feelings type.

He drove them through town and then out to the golf course, where a metal gate was across the road. The grounds were closed this time of year, but Cam put the SUV in park and got out, retrieving a key from his coat. The lock snicked open, and he pushed the gate out of the way, then got back in the SUV to drive through it.

"You have the key to the golf course."

"Being me has its advantages. I don't use my celebrity often, but tonight it came in handy."

Once they were through, he got out again and locked the gate. No one would disturb them.

He parked at the far end of the lot by the dark clubhouse. "Ready?"

She nodded. "I guess. What have you got up your sleeve?"

A quick smile, and he jumped out of the truck, then popped open the tailgate as she slammed her door and came around the bumper.

"Good heavens. What have you got in here?"

"Firewood, food, drinks, blankets to keep warm…"

Her eyes were huge. "Cam."

He was wearing gloves, but that didn't stop him from placing one along her cheek and looking into her eyes. "You said cozy fires and wine. You kind of left out stars, but they did come out for you tonight."

She looked up, sighed, and looked back at him. "You're crazy."

For you, he thought, but didn't say it. The thought alone was scary enough. "Come on. I'll get the fire started first and come back for the rest."

There was a fire pit just below the clubhouse, sometimes used in the summer time for special events. It wasn't your typical wheel-rim-in-the-ground kind of pit. Instead, it was stone and mortar, a lovely addition to the grounds, circled with stone-and-wood benches. Hannah sat on a bench while he arranged the wood and some little bits of kindling, then worked for a few moments making sure it lit and would stay lit. Little crackles snapped as the kindling caught, and he blew out a breath of relief. Once the blaze was established, he added a few logs to keep it going. Then he trotted back to the SUV and grabbed the picnic basket and blankets.

When he returned, Hannah was sitting on the bench, leaning forward toward the flames with her hands held out to the heat. He put down the basket, then unfolded one of the soft blankets and tucked it around her lap. "Okay?" he asked.

"This is so nice. I didn't think you'd take me this literally."

"I haven't done something like this for a long time, either." He sat on the bench beside her and reached for the picnic basket. "I'll confess, though, your friend Willow packed the basket. I figured she'd know your favorites."

"Oh Lord. Willow makes the best stuff. What's in there? I missed dinner."

He chuckled and opened the top. He frowned. "A dish of something brown, and a container of what looks like chips. And dessert for later."

"Mmm." Hannah grinned and peeked into the basket. "Willow's homemade hummus and pita chips. My fave."

He took those out first, and Hannah swiped a chip through the dip and held it to his lips. "Try it. She does a remarkable job."

He tasted it and liked it, so they munched on those a while as the fire crackled. He told Hannah about driving to Burlington to shop, and she shared how she hadn't found time to put up her tree yet. He poured warm mulled wine into a cup for her, and cider for himself, because he was driving. The spices teased his nostrils as he lifted the cup to his lips. The cider was perfect, delightfully appley and with mulled spices that made it sublime. He couldn't remember when he'd last had spiced cider or sat around a fire with a blanket. His life had been missing these simple pleasures for a long time.

"Oh, this is delicious." Hannah cupped her hands around her drink and tipped her face up to the sky. "Look at the stars, Cam. It's such a beautiful night."

The fire snapped and crackled, and Cam could hear the traffic from the highway faintly, the sound traveling on the clear air. "Good choice?" he asked.

She nodded, looking over at him. "It's the perfect date."

"Not perfect yet. Hang on."

He reached into the basket and took out a pair of

two-pronged forks. He twisted one and it extended to reach about three feet in length. He grinned and handed it to her. "Marshmallow forks. Dessert is s'mores."

Her laughter rang down over the first tee and into the valley. "S'mores. You really did think of everything."

Cam took out the bag of marshmallows, two bars of chocolate, and a package of graham crackers. While Hannah put a marshmallow on her stick, Cam got out two graham crackers and opened one of the chocolate bars, snapping it in half and placing it on the cracker.

Hannah toasted her marshmallow perfectly, and when she moved her stick over, Cam used the top cracker to sandwich the melty treat and pull it off the fork. He handed the finished s'more over to Hannah and took his fork, setting about toasting his own marshmallow.

Lips got sticky, and crumbs dropped onto the blankets, but neither of them seemed to care. Hannah finished her first one and took a healthy gulp of mulled wine before picking up her fork and stabbing another marshmallow. They had two each, then packed the detritus in the basket, which Cam put to the side after topping up their drinks.

"I've now eaten and had enough wine that the edges are getting a little fuzzy," Hannah said, putting her feet up on the bench and pulling the blanket around her.

"So you're cozy?"

"Very."

Cam got up and added wood to the fire, sending up a spray of sparks and renewed snapping as the birch bark caught and flickered. When he sat down again, he sat in a corner of the bench away from her and patted the empty space beside him. "Come on over here and curl up. We can watch the fire for a while."

She did, snuggling up next to him with her feet on the bench, and pulling the blanket over them both. Her head rested in the hollow of his shoulder, and he closed his eyes for a moment, enjoying the sensation. He'd missed this more than he liked to admit. Not wanting to have a serious relationship and also not fooling around with puck bunnies had left him leading a rather monastic existence. He put his arm around her and let out a long breath. He should confess his real reason for not doing the benefit. He wanted her to understand he wasn't just blowing it off or trying to buy his way in without putting in effort.

And he wanted to trust that she wouldn't judge him for it, or look at him differently.

"Hey, Han?"

"Mmmm hmmm?" Her reply was lazy and lovely, and it stirred things inside him he didn't know existed. His heart stuttered, afraid to be vulnerable, and yet somehow longing to connect with her on a deeper level. His throat tightened. What a time to realize he actually believed in love…and missed its presence in his life.

"I need to tell you something."

She twisted a little so she was looking up in his face. "Uh oh. This sounds serious."

"Not too serious," he replied, his heart thundering now. "It's just…there's a reason why I said no to the benefit. A reason I've never actually said out loud before."

She twisted farther and sat up a bit so she could look into his face better. "But you want to tell me?"

"I don't want you to think that I… Well, I don't know what you think. I gave you money, but I didn't give you my time, and I think that's what you really wanted."

Her eyes were bright. "I won't lie. I've wondered why you were so quick to say no and were equally quick to open your wallet."

Cam took a deep breath. It was now or never. "You wanted me to read a book at story time. And give a speech. But those things… Han, you couldn't have asked for two harder things. The truth is…" He swallowed against the lump of fear. "The truth is, I can't read very well."

She smiled. "I didn't realize you were a perfectionist. No one said you had to do a perfect job, Cam."

Oh God, she didn't get it. He tried again. "No, I mean…I've never been officially tested, but I think I'm dyslexic or something. The letters don't make sense all the time. It's like they move around or overlap. Or things like P and B and stuff get mixed up. I mean, I can do it. It's just hard, and I'm super slow. Same thing when it comes to my writing skills."

The smile had slipped from her face. "Cam. I had no idea. I'm sorry. I wouldn't have asked otherwise."

"It's not something I talk about."

She sat all the way up and faced him. "But…you got through school and everything."

"I got through because I was a hockey prodigy. I had a tutor. I scraped through most of my classes, and I'm pretty sure I got marked way up so I could keep playing. When you asked me to read to kids…" His voice caught, and he felt a hundred kinds of stupid. "Any of those kids would probably read better than me, you know? Some hero."

Her bright eyes had softened and looked into his. "You're not dumb, Cam. Having a learning disability doesn't mean you're stupid."

"Let's just say it doesn't feel that way."

"Fair enough."

He was glad she didn't try to dismiss his feelings. "Anyway, I wanted you to understand. I'm not trying to be selfish or unhelpful. If it was anything but reading…"

"It's okay. It really is. One of the librarians is going to do the story hour. What would be really great is if you'd go to the benefit dinner. Maybe even…with me."

He'd made it into the world of professional sports. He had a World Cup gold medal and had held the Stanley Cup. He'd been the NHL MVP twice. He should have confidence up the wazoo. Instead, he was sitting on a park bench in front of a fire feeling as uncertain as he ever had in his life.

"You want to go with me?"

"Of course I do." She put her hand on his arm. "Why wouldn't I?"

Because she was Hannah Freaking Gallagher, honor roll student and overachiever, the ungettable girl. And he was Cam Collier, dumb jock. But he didn't say that. Instead, he leaned forward and kissed her, a long, lingering kiss that warmed him from the inside out.

"You're so amazing," he murmured, pulling her into his arms and kissing her again.

They kissed for a long time, holding on to each other, letting the slow burn of desire keep them warm as the fire burned down. Eventually, they pulled back from the kiss, and he held her close as they looked at the stars poking through the inky blackness.

"Wow," she said quietly. "Good date, Collier. Top notch."

He chuckled. "It wasn't anything elaborate."

"It was just what I needed. And thank you for telling me the truth." She angled her head so she could look at him yet again. "You know you could get tested. Get some help."

"And have the world know I'm an idiot who can't read?"

"Again, you're not an idiot." She spun around and looked him dead in the eye. "If that little boy from The Purple Pig came up to you and said he had a learning disability, would you call him an idiot who can't read?"

He was horrified. "Of course not!"

"Well then, why would you talk to yourself that way?"

She was right, but it was impossible to change twenty-odd years of thinking like turning off a switch. "I know. I know. Except I don't, you know?"

Hannah nodded. "Sure I do. Let me just leave you with this. You could be a real inspiration to people with learning disabilities if you ever wanted to." He was about to protest when she lifted a hand. "I'm not pressuring you. It's just food for thought if you're ever ready."

He nodded, but the thought terrified him. "Right now, I just want to recover from this concussion and get back to my life."

The statement sobered them both. It had been a nearly perfect evening, but there wouldn't be many of these before he had to go back to his life. He tried to imagine being in a relationship with Hannah and being across the country while she was here. It seemed impossible. But imagining her leaving Darling behind to take a chance on him was even more impossible. Her business was here. Her family and stakes in other businesses... She was so entrenched in this community, how could he ever ask her to leave?

And he couldn't retire. He was only twenty-nine. He wasn't ready to give up hockey, and what if they tried it and it didn't work?

But the thought of leaving her behind after Christmas made his heart hurt. It wasn't the same as it had been with Alyssa. He'd loved her, but Hannah... There was already history with her. Their lives were already intertwined in a strange and wonderful way. He wasn't saying he was in love with her, but he cared about her so much.

"You're thinking so hard that smoke is going to start coming out of your ears," Hannah said softly, picking up his hand in hers. "Don't try to figure everything out. And this is coming from someone who plans everything. I don't want to analyze us out of what we might be able to have for a few short weeks. I want to be with you, Cam. I know what this is. But it feels good and right and dammit, we deserve it, don't we?"

He squeezed her fingers. "Someone once told you you didn't deserve it, huh? Who is he? I'll tune him up."

She laughed lightly. Their knees were pressed together, and he loved every single spot where their bodies connected. "You can't beat up everyone. But his name was Liam. He didn't like having a strong woman for a partner. I made him look bad."

Cam snorted. "His stupid loss, then. Because you're incredible. Any guy would be so lucky to have you. You are smart, savvy, dedicated, kind, beautiful… He should have been proud of you, not threatened."

He wasn't expecting tears to fill her eyes, but they glowed in the firelight and shone on her lashes. "Hey, don't cry."

"All the things he used to deride me for, you are proud of. It's so different and great."

"Maybe because we're more alike than we knew, Han. We see what we want, and we go after it. Not by stepping on others, but by working hard and demanding a lot of ourselves." He kissed the tip of her nose. "I like you a lot, but damn, I respect you even more. And that's something new for me."

She nodded quickly, and one tear splashed down off her lashes. "Have you wished that this didn't have to be just Christmas?" she asked and then bit down on her lip, as if unsure if she should have asked the question.

"Yeah, I have. But your life is here, and mine is there. Let's just do that live-in-the-moment thing again."

In response, she shifted and straddled his lap, then kissed him until his brain blanked of all other thoughts than just her. And when the fire burned down, they packed up their gear, threw a bucket of snow on the dying embers, and left the golf course.

10

F or the second time, Hannah woke with Cam in the bed beside her. This time he was awake, his dark eyes watching her, and she smiled as she stretched.

"Well, hello."

"Good morning."

She couldn't remember a time when she'd been this happy in…forever. "How's your head? Better job pacing yourself?"

They'd taken their time last night, and it had been… Well, transcendent sounded cheesy, but it was pretty accurate. She'd been thoroughly loved, and she'd given as good as she got.

"I feel like a million bucks," he confirmed, and reached over beneath the blankets and pulled her closer. "Slept like the dead, too. You're good for me, Hannah Banana."

"Ditto." She ran her hand through his hair, loving the softness, even though one spot stuck up stubbornly.

"By the way, thank you for not going in for *the flow* hair that so many players have. Or the gross beards, either."

He laughed. "You don't like facial hair?"

"A little is okay. I just can't see how a full beard can be comfortable when you're getting all sweaty and wearing a helmet."

"I don't like it, either. Besides, I gotta keep the baby face for the ladies."

In response, she ran her hand over his rough jaw. He had stubble there now from overnight, but she didn't mind. A little was sexy.

"What do you want to do today? I have an open house with a client tomorrow, but I'm free as a bird all day." She wasn't going to worry about the benefit next weekend. Everything was in place. Surely she deserved one day off?

"Let's put up your Christmas tree. I'll help."

"Really?" She sat up, clutching the covers to her chest. "You want to put up my tree?"

"Sure, why not?"

Hannah loved Christmas. All the siblings had always gathered to put up the tree at their parents' place. But over the past few years, her brothers had started traditions with their own families. Rory and Oaklee were celebrating their first Christmas in their house. Laurel and Aiden had started their family, and Willow and Ethan had three kids at their house. Priorities changed. Sure, Cait and Claire were still home, but Hannah's mom and dad had put up their tree on Monday night and not said anything to anyone about it. The changes had chipped away at her Christmas spirit. But today, she could get a tree with Cam and put it up and do all the fun things in her own house.

"Oh my God, I'm so excited." She jumped out of bed, not caring that she was naked. "Let's grab coffee at The Purple Pig and then get a tree at the garden center and—"

"Wow. I had no idea this was so thrilling for you."

"Putting up a tree alone is a sad affair. But you're here. Let's do it."

They had a quick shower since Hannah could still smell the smoke from their campfire in her hair. Today, she didn't care about looking perfect, so she rolled her damp hair in a low bun and plopped a cute hat on her head to keep it warm. Jeans, ankle boots, and an old jacket rounded out the ensemble. If there was any pitch on the tree, she didn't want to get it on her good coat.

They stopped at the Pig and said hello to Emily, then took their coffee and headed to the Ladybug Garden Center. The manager, George, was doing a brisk business with trees, but it didn't take long for Hannah to pick the one she wanted. Then she went inside in search of Laurel, who would definitely be working on a busy Saturday before Christmas. Laurel was stacking cookies and squares on a rack inside the shop, a fresh delivery from a local bakery. During the holidays, the garden center did a booming business with decorations and seasonal treats.

"Hello!" Laurel brushed off her hands and moved forward to give Hannah a hug. "It feels like I haven't seen you in forever."

"Everyone's been busy. Including you. This place is hoppin'."

"Trees and wreaths and poinsettias, for sure. And the bakery started sending shortbread and all kinds of cookies and squares. I swear, no one has to do any Christmas baking at all. They even sent—" she held up a container. "—little jars of buckeyes."

"Sold." Hannah loved the chocolate and peanut butter treats. "We just came for a tree. Mine's not up yet."

"We?"

Hannah met Laurel's gaze. "Me and…Cam."

Laurel's eyes twinkled in response. "Oh, honey. Yee haw."

Hannah burst out laughing. "Stop that! Someone will hear you."

"Oh, whatever. But seriously, you can't even give me juicy deets, because there's too many people, and it's crazy in here." She peered closer into Hannah's face. "There are juicy deets, right?"

Hannah didn't answer, but she felt the heat of a blush rush into her cheeks.

"Ho damn," Laurel said on a low breath. "When's our next girls' night?"

"I am not going to kiss and tell," Hannah said firmly. "That's not my style."

"Well, clearly not with Oaklee. She doesn't need to know that about her brother. Gross. But, Hannah, whatever is going on looks good on you. So yeah, enjoy it."

"I intend to. Now, I was hoping to grab a few things

before I go. Including these." She held up the container. "I'm gonna go. We're all set for next weekend?"

"Sure thing. Centerpieces will be ready and delivered Saturday morning, and you already have my silent auction contribution. Aiden and I bought our tickets to the dinner, too. Your mom and dad offered to keep all the kids so all of us can go."

Hannah's heart warmed. That was one thing about the Gallaghers. When something was going on, they had each other's backs. "So everyone will be there?"

She nodded. "All your siblings, anyway. Your folks are going to go to the afternoon events."

An unexpected calm descended over Hannah. For weeks, she'd been stressed about this event, but the truth was, her family was solidly behind her. The town was, too. It was all going to be fine. She felt more love and support in this moment than she'd felt in many years.

Maybe, just maybe, it was okay for Hannah to be Hannah.

Cam ventured into the small store, then smiled at Hannah as he caught her with Laurel. "Hey, the tree's all ready to go. You had a blanket in your truck, so I put it on the roof rack and put the tree on top so you don't scratch any of the paint."

"Hey, Cam."

"Laurel. You're doing big business today."

"It's Christmas. The season of joy and happiness." She smiled brightly at him, and a blush crept up his cheeks.

"Oh God," he muttered.

"Sorry. Or maybe more…sorry not sorry. It's kind of cute seeing you blush."

"Please don't bring this up with Aiden or Ethan or Rory. I'm not ready for the third degree from protective brothers."

"Aw, come on. I mean, just because one's a fire-fighter, the other's a cop, and the third is a vet, who is around all sorts of lethal medications…why worry?"

He chuckled. "Ha, ha."

One of the cashiers waved at Laurel, so she gave a parting grin. "I gotta go. You two have a brilliant day."

Hannah held the container of buckeyes in her hand and looked at Cam. "Pick something from the rack, and we'll have it with coffee this afternoon."

"Oooh, I get to pick a treat?" He rubbed his hands together, and she laughed.

He chose something she didn't expect: a Christmas Stollen, heavy and dense with marzipan and coated with powdered sugar. It was one of her favourites, too, and not overly sweet, beyond the marzipan, of course. She added it to the buckeyes and a roll of wired ribbon from the wreath section and went to the cash register. Before long, they were on their way back to her house, smelling of spruce needles and holiday spirit.

Cam unloaded the tree while Hannah went to her basement to retrieve her tree stand and decorations at the bottom of the stairs. She'd already moved the furni-ture aside so she could put the tree in the corner by the fireplace, and by the time Cam wrestled the thing through the door, she had the stand ready and waiting.

With a flurry and fluff of branches, the trunk settled

into the stand. Hannah held the tree steady while Cam knelt down and tightened the wingnuts to hold it perfectly straight. When he was done, he got up, stood back, and gave a whistle. "Good choice on the tree. It's perfect."

She thought so, too. Even more because he was here with her. It felt like a very couple-ish thing to do. She wasn't going to analyze it too deeply, either. She was going to enjoy the day.

"Hang on," she said, and disappeared to the kitchen. She came back with her phone and started a holiday playlist, which she put through a portable speaker on the fireplace mantle. "Gotta have some carols while we're decorating."

The playlist was a Christmas Classics one, so right after Burl Ives, Perry Como came on. After turning on the gas fireplace, she gave Cam the tree skirt to put underneath and started unpacking the decorations.

"Lights first," she said, taking out several bundles. They were rolled around flat pieces of cardboard to keep them from tangling, and she tested each set and made sure it was working before handing them to Cam, who could reach the tall branches and around the back better than she could. As she opened a pack of replacement bulbs, she stole a look at him. It seemed impossible that he was here, in her living room, helping her put up a Christmas tree. Tree decorating was an intimate thing, when she thought about it. It was usually an activity for families or couples, or at the very least, people who were very special to each other. Was Cam special to her? Maybe he shouldn't be, but he was. He fiddled with a branch, and a lump formed in Hannah's throat. He was a good man. And she was beginning to care about him —a lot. Not just because they knew each other, but in other, deeper ways.

But she could not fall for him. She couldn't. He was leaving soon. This was a short-term thing she would look back on with fond memories and nostalgia. Right?

"Got the next set ready?"

Cam's voice pulled her out of her thoughts, and she immediately pasted on a smile. "Oh, sorry! I got distracted."

"Really."

If he knew the direction of her thoughts, he'd be out the door faster than she could say "penalty box." She brightened her smile and said, "Yeah. I was looking at your ass."

His eyebrows lifted, and he left the tree to come over to where she was sitting with the bundle of lights in her lap. Her heart hammered as he neared, but he merely reached down and took the lights from her hands.

Her breath escaped with relief.

Except Cam put the lights down on the coffee table and came back, braced his hands on the arms of the chair, and leaned in to kiss her.

It was no chaste peck. Even though he kept his hands to himself, his mouth did lots of talking all on its own. It wooed and persuaded, tasted and devoured, until Hannah was ready to forget all about the tree and start losing clothes.

Then he stepped back, retrieved the lights, and went to put them on the tree.

"I, uh…what was that for?"

"For staring at my ass."

"If I do it again, do I get double the punishment?"

He laughed and roped the lights around the middle of the tree. "Sweetheart, the kiss wasn't the punishment. Walking away was."

Damn him. Hannah smiled to herself and reached for another set of lights.

After the lights, they put garland on in swoops, and then Hannah's ornaments, which were all in red, green, and gold. The final touch was the star for the top. Hannah's tree lights were all white, and the star was gold and trimmed with white LED lights and glittering crystals. She'd paid a lot of money for it and kept it in the original box when not in use. She handed it to Cam, and he situated it on the top of the tree, and then they stepped back and admired their handiwork.

"I like it," she said softly.

"Me, too," he said. He stood behind her and wrapped his arms around her middle, and the bottom of his chin rested against her temple. It was an intimate moment, admiring their tree.

"Are you glad you came home?"

"More every day."

"Cam…"

He turned her to face him and cupped her jaws in his hands, his thumbs resting on her cheeks. "I know the future is… Well, not this. But I'm not sorry, Hannah. I'll never be sorry. Being with you has been so good."

Tears stung the backs of her eyes. "For me, too."

"I've been lonely a long time," he admitted.

She had, too. Longer than she cared to admit. Maybe too long, because she was probably being foolish right now. She should send him on his way before someone got hurt. But she couldn't. She physically could not form the words. And that, more than anything, scared her to death.

11

Cam kissed her lips gently, his heart pounding with both anticipation and trepidation. He was walking a very fine line right now. There was something about Hannah that just got to him. Maybe it was the way she laughed, or how she was so very capable but hid a vulnerability he understood more than she could imagine. She hadn't been staring at his ass earlier, either. He'd seen the look on her face as her hands stilled over the lights, and he'd known.

This fling might be too much for her. For both of them. Especially since it didn't feel like a fling at all.

Not to him, anyway.

She responded, melting against him as he sank his fingers into her hair. He loved her hair, the wild, thick, red mass of it cascading over his hands as she moaned into his mouth. She was so responsive, something he hadn't imagined when he'd first encountered her that day at The Purple Pig. How had he ever thought she was uptight? She was pliant and willing in his arms right now.

"Hannah," he whispered roughly.

"Cameron," she replied, and that was it. The husky way she said his full name—no one ever called him by that—reached in and did something to him that couldn't be undone.

The light had dimmed in the late afternoon, and now the light was provided by the glow of the tree and the flicker of the fireplace. It danced on her face, darkening her eyes and highlighting the hollow of her throat as she tipped her head back. He kissed the base of her throat and licked up her neck, feeling her shiver with pleasure.

He wanted to give her that; undiluted, magnificent pleasure. Slowly, he pulled her sweater over her head, then cupped her breast in his hand, loving the feel of the hard tip as it pressed against his palm. She pulled at his hoodie, and he made short work of pulling it off and dropping it on the floor. Next to go was her bra, and then he picked her up and lay her down on the plush sofa, her body sinking into the cushions beneath him. Her hands were above her head, and he made the most of the invitation as he tasted her breasts before kissing her again.

And still they didn't rush. They savored each touch and taste until the need for satisfaction grew too strong. Cole got up and removed his jeans, then leaned over and removed Hannah's until she was stretched out naked on the sofa.

The light from the fireplace cast shadows that licked

her golden skin and shone against her burnished hair. Cole had enough presence of mind to reach for a condom in his jeans pocket, and then he was inside her, feeling her arch against him, hearing her breath as she gasped and moved in rhythm with him. He upped his pace, resting most of his weight on one elbow while he used his opposite thumb to flick her nipple. She cried out, and he adjusted, bracing himself on his hands so that he could lick them the way she needed.

"Oh God. Cam. Cam."

She said his name. She hadn't done that before, and an overwhelming emotion washed over him. Her legs wrapped around his waist, her strong thighs cinching him close, and he pushed harder, her cries urging him on. When she finally came apart around him, he was certain he had never felt this sort of victory ever in his life—and that was saying something. Her hips pulsed against him, and her voice was a hoarse sob as the climax pounded through her, and with it went his last bit of control.

He looked down at her as he came, her dazed eyes staring up at him, and he knew he was in serious, serious trouble.

He'd gone and fallen in love with Hannah Gallagher.

THERE WAS NO WAY HE COULD TELL HER HOW HE FELT.

Cam held on to his feelings tightly over the next few days. After decorating the tree, they made dinner together, then curled up in front of the fire and talked for hours before going to bed. On Sunday, they went to her parents' house for Sunday dinner, where he was completely included, and no one—not even Rory—said a thing about him being there with Hannah. It was almost as if they'd all been forewarned…which he figured they had been. It didn't matter. He enjoyed roast beef and all the fixings, lots of laughs, and Moira's top-notch apple pie. He'd spent a lot of time in the Gallagher house as a boy. It had felt good to be at home there again.

Monday, Hannah was back at work, but he had an appointment in Montpelier anyway. That night he cooked for her—fresh pasta in a Bolognese sauce and salad. Tuesday, he helped her go through her lists for the auction. And Wednesday, he decreed she needed a few hours off and to grab her skates.

He hadn't been on the ice since his injury, but as they sat on a bench on the bank of Fisher Creek, he shoved his feet in his skates, and it felt a lot like home. Blades were as natural to him as a favourite pair of sneakers. They shoved guards over the blades as they made their way to the frozen creek, and then they took off the guards and left them on the bank.

He pushed off, felt the ice beneath his feet, and nearly cried. God, he'd missed this. It had only been a few weeks, but he'd missed it like crazy.

Hannah wasn't quite as sure on hers, but she pushed away from the bank and with shortened strides, made it to where he was waiting for her.

"I'm feeling a bit outmatched," she said, her breath

forming clouds. The lights along the walking path cast a soft light on the creek. Farther down, toward the garden center, the creek was wider, and he could hear children laughing. Hannah's nose was pink from the cold, her blue eyes bright and shining beneath a soft knitted cap. How had he not seen how extraordinary she was?

It was going to kill him to leave her. Yet what choice did he have?

"Come on," he said softly, and held out his gloved hand.

She was wearing mittens that matched her hat, and she folded her smaller hand into his. Together, they skated up the creek, Cam slowing to match her speed, which smoothed out as she went along.

They skated along, past the memorial, under the Kissing Bridge, and up toward the traffic bridge that connected one side of town to the other. Hannah's strides were stronger now, and he let go of her hand and skated off, enjoying the freedom, indulging in some footwork, laughing from the sheer joy of it. He wasn't ready to give this up. Not yet. All he was missing was a stick in his hand and a puck on the blade.

Hannah goofed around a bit, too, going around him in circles, doing little half-jumps. She grabbed his hand, performing a twirl that took her right into his arms.

"Hmm," he said, looking down at her lips. "Look at you."

"I'm so rusty," she said on a laugh. "But I'm never going to be like you on skates, so I might as well embrace my mediocrity and enjoy myself."

He pulled her close. "You, my Hannah Banana, will

never be mediocre. Never let anyone tell you otherwise, and never hide it."

"Cam…"

"Right." He pushed her away, spun her around, and put his hands on her hips. "You leading the train, Ms. Gallagher?"

She burst out laughing. "There are two of us. That means I'm the engine and you're the caboose."

"Someone's gotta be."

She started to skate, and he matched his strides to hers, working together to make their way down the ice. She surprised him by doing a half turn and skating backward so they were face-to-face. He captured one of her hands, leaving his other on her hip, and grinned.

"What are you doing?" she asked, still skating with strong, even strides.

"Dancing. Hush, and let me lead."

He was no figure skater, but he was nimble enough that he led her through a couple of turns so that he was the one skating backward, taking her with him. As they reached the Kissing Bridge again, he slowed and pulled her in so their bodies were pressed together and she was no longer skating, just sliding forward from his momentum. He clasped her hand tightly, put his wide palm along the hollow of her back, and slowed until they were making tiny circular steps on the ice.

She sighed and rested her head against his shoulder.

"Hannah…"

He stopped moving altogether and kissed her, right there on the ice under the Kissing Bridge, hidden from view. He wanted to make love to her right now, not because of burning need or desire, but because he longed to feel that connection with her again. It both scared and thrilled him. Was this how love felt? Was this love as a grown up? It certainly made all his other feelings pale in comparison.

He loved her. He wasn't sure how to tell her, but he wanted to. Wasn't sure if it was even fair to say the words and then walk away, but it felt wrong somehow not to.

"Hannah, I…"

"What is it?"

The words tangled in his throat. It wasn't the right time. Maybe it would never be the right time. Instead, he leaned forward and kissed her forehead. "I'm glad I came home for Christmas," he said softly, then closed his eyes. Going back to Denver was going to be harder than he ever imagined.

HANNAH LET OUT A SLOW BREATH AND LET CAM FOLD her into his arms. What had he been going to say? He'd been different since Saturday, though she couldn't quite pinpoint how or why. There'd been a naturalness to them being together that hadn't happened before. Even at dinner the other night with her family, he'd struck a fine balance of hanging with the family and yet being… coupley. A look across the table, coming up behind her in the kitchen and putting a hand on her waist, even bringing her a second cup of tea while they watched hockey highlights.

She cared about him a lot. Another time, another

place, maybe it would go somewhere. But she was rather glad he'd said he was happy he'd come home and not made any sort of declaration.

She didn't want him to love her. She just wanted to enjoy this time, be able to hold it close in the months ahead when she got lonely again. As she certainly would. Cam once made the comment that she was "ungettable." She supposed that translated to high-maintenance. Was she? She didn't think so.

She clung to his jacket and enjoyed the hug. She wasn't ungettable. What she was, was afraid. Afraid of changing herself, afraid of no one loving her as she was. She stayed in Darling because despite being an achiever, she was not a risk-taker. She could be a big fish in a little pond here. She didn't know how to be a little fish. And it made her admire Cam a little more, knowing that over the years he'd had to work to become a big fish, against a lot of odds and without his family close by. He was so much braver than she was.

Being a big fish meant she was lonely. But at least she wasn't lonely in the middle of the unknown.

Damn Cam for coming to town and making her face that vulnerability.

And damn him for making her feel so alive she was reminded of what she was missing because of the choices she'd made.

12

He was headed back to Denver right after Christmas.

The go-ahead came from the doctor in Montpelier in a follow-up appointment on Friday, and Cam now sat on the back deck, huddled in his winter jacket, frowning at his mixed feelings.

This was what he wanted. To go back, get into training again, return to the ice and the team. And yet the thought of leaving Hannah behind left a hollow feeling in his gut. Saying goodbye was going to be awful. Not just the situation and the actual saying of it, but the walking away and going through his days knowing she was so far away. The end of what they'd only just begun.

The sun was just beginning to creep through the trees, and Cam took a big breath. Today was the benefit, and he was going to help Hannah and Oaklee as much as he could. Oaklee was going to be handling the activities in town during the day, while Hannah was manning banquet HQ at the golf club. He'd given her the details

of the trip he was offering in the auction, and she'd
done up some sort of display for it. She'd asked if he
could meet her at the clubhouse at ten to help her make
sure everything was on schedule and perfect.

The sliding door opened and his mom came out,
bundled in a fleece jacket of his dad's and carrying two
cups of coffee. "You're out here early."

"Just doing some thinking."

"About Hannah Gallagher?"

He nodded. "Yeah. And other things."

"You got in a little over your head, huh."

He laughed and accepted the steaming coffee.
"Yeah, I guess I did."

She sat down on a cold chair and sighed. "Well,
you're almost thirty years old. I couldn't expect you to
stay in your childhood bed forever. You've been gone a
lot of nights."

"She's…really special."

"Of course she is. Beautiful and smart and successful. I don't know what the guys around here have been
staying away for."

"Because they're idiots," he grumbled, and sipped
his coffee. "She's got her own insecurities. She's not a
ballbuster. Even if some people think she is."

"Maybe she just needed someone strong enough to
go toe to toe with her," his mother said wisely. "And you
are that, my stubborn son. So maybe this concussion
turned out to be a bit of a blessing."

He frowned and didn't say anything for several long
moments. Finally, he looked over at her. "But what now?
Mom, I'm going back on the twenty-seventh. I got the

all clear to at least practice. I have to go. I have a responsibility to be there. I *want* to be there."

Her face was sad as she looked over at him. "And Hannah's life is here."

"Her family. Her business. Her friends. How can I ask her to leave that behind? We've been together what, three weeks?" He made a scoffing sound and shook his head. "It's crazy."

"Does she love you as much as you love her?"

Her simple question rattled him. His gaze darted up and held hers, as fear and elation rushed together through his system. "I never said I loved her."

"You don't have to. It's all over your face and in the way you talk about her. Besides, you've known Hannah for years. It's not like you just met."

It wasn't, and she was right. It was more like taking an old relationship and shifting it, molding it like clay into something new and beautiful.

"It's not an easy thing to say. And what would be the point?"

She patted his hand. "The world would be a lot better place if people would just say 'I love you' more often instead of holding it inside. Loving someone is a gift. You should tell her."

He was quiet a little longer, and she leaned closer so she could peer into his face. "What is it? What are you afraid of?"

He swallowed against a lump in his throat. "What if I say it, and she doesn't feel the same? What if..." His voice trailed away. "Aw, hell, Mom. I don't even know what I want this to look like, but I'm pretty sure she's not going to go for it. It's a lot to ask of a person. I don't even know what the next five years of my life are going to look like. How do I drag her into that?"

"Why would you have to drag anyone? Life is always one choice after another. It would suck if you didn't at least give her the chance to say yes to something great. Maybe she's feeling the same way and doesn't know how to tell you, too. I hate to tell you this, Cam, but with matters of the heart, it comes down to making yourself vulnerable and taking chances."

He wasn't a stranger to taking chances. Heck, his whole career was based on it. But it was different when his heart was involved. He'd been through this before, and it had hurt, a lot. It would be exponentially worse with Hannah. He was older, wiser, and a lot more scared.

And yet he knew, deep down, his mom was right. The only way this was going to work was if he laid it all out there. As if she sensed he was working through the puzzle of his thoughts, his mom stood and patted his shoulder before going back inside.

Hannah had said enough about her past for him to know that people expected a lot of her. Words wouldn't be enough for her; he needed to show her how important she was to him. And he knew there was one way he could do it, if he was brave enough.

But first, he needed to grab some breakfast and prepare to convert the clubhouse into a winter fairy tale. Then he'd sort it all out.

· · ·

HANNAH WAS FEELING ALL SORTS OF JITTERS, BUT THEY were the good kind. Last year had been the inaugural year of the benefit, and this year she'd made a few changes to simplify the setup, and it wasn't all new. Besides, she had a good feeling. Nothing was going to go wrong today. Oaklee was popping into each sponsoring business to make sure their donation boxes and raffles were running smoothly, then checking in at the library to help with the story hour and used book sale. Hannah had already been into The Purple Pig and got a hot chocolate and a cookie. A dollar from each sale today was going to support the cause. Even Papa Luigi's pizza was putting on a special deal over the lunch hour for a slice and a soda, and an extra dollar paid for a ticket in a draw for a New Year's Eve pizza feast. Rory had said he was buying a ton of tickets so they could have the food for their New Year's party all figured out.

She had a clipboard and a handful of volunteers, all busily setting up banquet tables and chairs. She'd rented the linens, and they were pressed and waiting to be placed on tables. There was a podium at the front for announcements by the emcee, a local radio personality who had donated his time.

Boxes lined the back, full of silent-auction donations ready to be displayed. And she had six hours to do it all. Then she could rush back home and change out of her jeans and sweater and into the killer cocktail dress she'd bought for tonight. It wasn't a black-tie event, but it was semi-formal, and she wanted to knock Cam's eyeballs out.

Speaking of, the man himself strode through the

door, carrying a tray with coffee and a paper bag nestled between the cups. "Wow. Ready to give this room a makeover?"

She laughed. "You have no idea." She swept out her hand. "I have some volunteers to help with the room setup, and you, mister…" She smiled up at him. "I've got twinkly light kinds of things for you to do."

"Coffee first?"

"God, yes."

He handed her a cup and then leaned down and kissed her lightly. "I'm not really into PDAs, but I wanted to do that," he murmured, pulling back. A quick glance showed a few of the ladies staring, and he smiled shyly. "Oops."

"Oh, it's not like this town hasn't been talking anyway." She grinned at him over top of her cup. "Besides, you're my date tonight."

"That's right. I washed my special sweatpants for the occasion."

"Ha, ha."

He'd also brought breakfast sandwiches, which she was thankful for, because she'd had sugar for breakfast between the hot chocolate and the cookie. They took ten minutes to eat, and then she showed him where the decorations were and what she wanted to do with them. "The white trees have LED lights on them. The idea is to do a group of three on either side of the podium and make it a little magical. There should be extension cords in the boxes. And someone from the garden center should be here anytime with centerpieces and extra poinsettias."

"Great. All under control."

"I'm going to put the linens on the display tables and start setting up auction items. Sound okay?"

"Of course."

She left him then, but she stole glances at him as he moved around setting up the trees, plugging them in and rearranging them again. She had several donations for the auction, and she put his in the very center as the big draw—the trip to the Stanley Cup final. The Foxborough Inn had donated a weekend stay-and-dine getaway, Willow had offered up ten yoga classes, and even Rory had put together a healthy pet-care package filled with treats, toys, and a certificate for a pet checkup and vaccinations. The donations went on and on, and Hannah's heart warmed as she put one after another on the tables, along with the description and bidding sheet for each.

There was even a beautiful crocheted baby blanket by Amelia Evans, who had been Hannah's mother's school teacher, and who must now be at least eighty. The work was precise and perfect, done in a pale yellow, like liquid sunshine. Hannah ran her fingers over the delicate yarn and felt a wistful tug at her heart. What would she ever do with a blanket like this? She probably wouldn't ever have kids. The clock had begun to tick softly a few years ago.

"Wow, that's pretty." Cam's voice sounded at her ear, and she jumped a little, pulling her hand away.

"Yeah. Did you know Amelia taught my mom? And yet here she is, still finding the time to donate something for this charity."

"As a teacher, she probably appreciates the cause," he said. "So what do you think?"

She turned around and smiled, enchanted. "Oh, Cam. Who knew you'd have an artistic eye?"

He'd placed the trees perfectly and plugged them in so the lights glowed at the front of the room. Then he'd somehow taken the rest of the little lights and twined them with the greenery that hung around the door to the banquet room, making it sparkle. "I wish I had more to do something around perimeter of the room, you know?"

"No, this is perfect. Laurel's centerpieces are going to look after extra sparkle, don't you worry. The lighting is going to be perfect."

She'd just said the words when Aiden stuck his head in the door. "Shrubbery!"

Hannah rolled her eyes and then burst out laughing as Aiden and Cam went through a Monty Python bit about shrubberies. Before long, the two of them were lugging in the centerpieces and poinsettias. Hannah rushed to get a tablecloth, and when the last of the delivery was inside, she grabbed Cam's arm and pulled him over.

"Okay, so look at this. Laurel came up with the design, and George put them together." George had, until the last year or so, been a homeless veteran on Darling's streets. Now he was Laurel's manager and lived with his girlfriend, Lindsay, right here in town.

Precisely in the middle of the table, she put a two-inch thick circle of wood. On top of that went a small wreath that George had made, and in the middle was a glass candle holder and a thick, white candle inside. "Each table will have one of these. There are fifteen tables. Add these with the rest of the lights, and the ones I have to intersperse on the auction tables, and it'll be magical in here."

The volunteers were nearly done setting up the chairs at each table, and then the caterers arrived. Hannah disappeared to direct them to the clubhouse kitchen, and when she looked out again, Cam was snapping a tablecloth and letting it fall onto the table, then adjusting it with a critical eye. One of the volunteers said something to him, and he laughed, answered, and worked together with them to make sure everything was just right.

How lucky was she, anyway? This had to be some sort of Christmas miracle. And it would be over as soon as the season was over, but for right now, it was pretty amazing.

He was amazing. Way more than she'd realized the day he'd said he wouldn't read at the library. He'd succeeded despite what she suspected was a significant learning disability. He'd risen to the top in competitive sport, in a way thousands of young players only dreamed.

Cam Collier was a special, special man.

"Ms. Gallagher?" One of the catering staff needed her attention, so she dragged her gaze away and turned to help.

She could think about their relationship later. Right now, she had to keep the day running on schedule. She didn't have time to worry about anything else.

13

Cam buttoned the suit jacket and smoothed the lapels. He was no stranger to tailored suits. They were regular game-day attire, and he made sure they fit him well. He'd paired the dark-gray suit with brown shoes and a shirt in the lightest shade of blue. He knotted the tie and tightened it, then ran his hands through his hair and shrugged.

He wasn't sure he was ready for tonight, but there came a time in a man's life that he couldn't run anymore. That something became important enough to stand for. Or someone, rather. That was Hannah for him. He wanted to try to make this work. Surely they could come to some kind of compromise? He could come back to Darling over the summer. Maybe she could travel to Denver now and again during the season.

Anything but saying goodbye.

And he knew that to convince a woman like Hannah, he needed to not just say the words, but show her how much she meant to him.

Just thinking about it made his stomach twist with anxiety. He'd almost rather get knocked in the head again, but he would do this. For her. For them. And to be a better person than he'd been in the past.

The parking lot at the golf club was already filling up when he arrived. Hannah had insisted on meeting him there, since she would be going a bit early to ensure everything was perfect and to be on hand when people started arriving. He stepped inside the banquet room, and soft, jazzy Christmas music met his ears. A bar was set up in the corner—that was an addition since he'd left at two—and a tuxedoed bartender was mixing drinks and pouring wine.

He didn't see Hannah yet, but he knew she had to be here. Instead, he zeroed in on Rory and Oaklee. His sister looked stunning in a red cocktail dress, and Rory was practically beaming.

"Well, you two clean up nice." He leaned over and kissed Oaklee's cheek. "How did the afternoon go?"

"Perfectly! The weather was amazing, so we had great crowds on Main, and I think there were maybe fifty kids at story hour. It looks like the individual efforts paid off, too. The used table was doing a booming business, and Papa Luigis could barely keep up with pizza orders. Hannah's thrilled."

"Speaking of, have you seen her?"

Oaklee shrugged. "Yes, but she disappeared a few minutes ago. I'll go see if I can find her."

Oaklee kissed Rory's cheek and slipped away. Rory's smile slipped a little, and he met Cam's gaze.

"Tonight's the night, man. After the benefit, because

we're all dressed up. I've got champagne in the fridge, and I'm gonna pop the question."

Cam grinned widely. "Look at you, scared shitless. Way to go, man. It's not every day that a guy gains a brother who is also his best friend."

Rory laughed a little. "Yeah, well, I know you've been hanging around my sister. Should I grill you about your intentions?"

This time, it was Cam's grin that faded. "Ask me after tonight," he said quietly."

Rory's jaw dropped. "Oh my God. You're not proposing…"

"No, of course not!" Cam's heart nearly stopped. "It's all too new. But… Well, Hannah and I just need to talk, you know?"

"You're smitten."

Cam raised an eyebrow. "Very."

"My sister is a handful."

"And a half."

Rory laughed then, a genuine, happy laugh. "Don't hurt her. But damn, bro…I can't think of anyone better to handle her shenanigans."

"God, I need a beer. I can't believe you said shenanigans."

They were just about to head to the bar when Hannah and Oaklee came through the door.

Cam's heart stuttered.

Oaklee was beautiful, but Hannah… She was incandescent. Her gold-sequined dress sparkled and glittered in the flickering light, modest in its cut, but stunning in its fit. Her hair was down, the whole fiery length of it curled about her shoulders.

"You are in so much trouble, dude," Rory said, clapping him on the shoulder.

"Shit," Cam answered.

Rory disappeared, and Cam met Hannah's gaze across the room. She gave him a slow smile and a wink, and he knew he was in way over his head. He ignored the stares and hellos aimed his way as he crossed the room, never breaking eye contact. And when he finally reached her, she put her hand on his arm and kissed his cheek while he caught his breath.

"You... Wow, Hannah. Just...wow."

"You like it?"

"I could say something like how it makes me want to get you out of it, but that's not true. I want to enjoy the whole evening, knowing the most gorgeous woman in the room is my date." He reached down and took her fingers in his. "When a candle burns this brightly, you want to stay close to it, you know?"

"Cam..."

"Let's enjoy the evening. Everything is in place, and according to Oaklee, today has been a booming success. Your hard work is over, Han."

And his was just beginning. He fought back the nerves that threatened to derail him.

They circulated together. Cam signed a few autographs, caught up with old teammates from his childhood days, and shook hands with the mayor and his wife. Hannah sipped on a glass of white wine while he indulged in a single beer. He had to drive later, and he also wanted his wits about him. Catering staff circulated with appetizers, and the mood was warm and festive as the dinner hour neared.

The emcee tapped on the mic and announced that dinner would begin in five minutes.

Hannah and Cam were seated at the front, along with the rest of the Gallaghers: Rory and Oaklee, Aiden and Laurel, and Ethan and Willow. Cait and Claire were at another table with their friends, but as Cam looked around, he was reminded of how wonderful this town was, as well as the Gallagher clan. He hadn't spent enough time with family over the years, but maybe now that would change.

The emcee opened the event with a welcome, and then invited Hannah to the podium. Cam smiled at her as she rose from her chair and made her way to the microphone.

"Good evening, everyone. Doesn't this place look beautiful? I'd like to thank all the volunteers who came out today to help with our setup and decorating, and also to so many who took part in our many activities throughout Darling today. I'm thrilled to announce that our preliminary numbers exceed that of last year, and we have a total of eleven thousand, two hundred and sixty-six dollars, all of which will go to our various literacy charities. Thank you so much for all your support!"

A round of loud applause followed, and as it died down, Hannah added, "If you haven't placed your bids on the auction items at the back, you can do so until eight p.m. Thank you again, and enjoy this wonderful dinner."

She made her way back down to her seat, and Cam noticed she didn't even look ruffled. Public speaking scared the hell out of him, but Hannah spoke with ease and authenticity. "You're amazing," he whispered, leaning over toward her as she sat.

"All this flattery is going to go to my head." She sent him a wry smile and reached for her water goblet.

"I hope so. You should realize how wonderful you are. And that people admire you for it."

Her blue gaze met his. "Cam."

"I mean it, Hannah. Screw anyone threatened by you. They're afraid of being eclipsed by the sun, but if they were smart, they'd bask in the glow."

To his surprise, her eyes glimmered with unshed tears. "Thank you," she whispered. "I needed to hear that."

He didn't say anything more, because he wanted to keep things easy for at least a little while longer. Instead, he reached over and squeezed her hand. Then they were served their entrée, and the banquet room echoed with the sounds of happy voices, cutlery, and soft music.

When their plates were removed and the candy-cane cheesecake was served, the emcee stepped up to the microphone again. Hannah's brow puckered, and she braced her feet as if to push back her chair, but Cam steadied her with a hand on her knee.

"Good evening again." The emcee's voice cut smoothly through the chatter, which immediately died down. "At this time, I'd like to invite Darling's favorite son, Cam Collier, to the podium."

He felt Hannah's gaze on his face, but he ignored it.

He couldn't look at her, or he wouldn't get through this. Instead, he stood, put his napkin on his chair, and went to the small stage.

The light was on him. He was no stranger to that. And no stranger to seeing a group of people before him, either. He wasn't a public speaker, but he wasn't shy. No, it was the subject matter that had him freaked out.

But he could do it. For Hannah.

"Good evening." He ran his hand through his hair and chuckled nervously. "Okay, so I'm going to be honest. I'm really nervous about being up here.

"Many of you have known me since I was a kid strapping on my first skates. I have a million great memories of growing up in this town. I played hockey at the rink, ate burgers and fries at the Sugarbush, and had my first legal drink at Suds." A few laughs came from the crowd and he grinned. "I went to school here, at least I did until I was sixteen, and my family is still here —my mom and dad, my sister Oaklee. And my 'other' family, too—the Gallaghers. If there are any stories about me as a kid, Rory's name is probably in there, too."

More laughter sounded in the room. But this was not the time to reminisce about boyish antics.

"But there is something you don't know about me," he said, and then cleared his throat. "It's something I've only ever told one person in my life. I've done a very good job of hiding it, and if anyone ever suspected, they kept it to themselves or pretended it didn't exist. The truth is…I am not a good reader."

He let out a breath, then continued. "When I say

I'm not a good reader, I don't mean that I'm a bit slow or I don't like it. I mean I have trouble with transposing and confusing letters, so I often miss the meaning of what I'm trying to read, or I give up because it takes me so long. I use the term 'not a good reader' because I have never been tested or evaluated. There are two reasons for that. One, I was afraid someone would find out, and I wouldn't be able to play hockey anymore. And two, I'm fairly certain now that some people did know, or at least suspect, and they pushed me through my schooling because I was good at putting a puck in a net."

He met Hannah's gaze. Her eyes were wide and her lower lip was quivering, and his throat tightened.

"Now I've made a career of doing just that. And I stayed quiet because I was ashamed and felt…stupid."

He smiled at Hannah. "But you know, it took a good knock to the head to bring me home. And when I got here, Hannah was determined I would help out with this benefit. I disappointed her when I refused to read at the library today. I was still ashamed of my secret, you see. In my head, I was that ten-year-old boy again, terrified of being called on to read in class, afraid that I'd start, and the kids would laugh at me. I have a great life. But I still have insecurities.

"I wish someone would have intervened with me earlier. Teachers told my parents that I struggled and my mom read with me every night. I went to extra help, but it wasn't enough. I wish that there had been a program for me, or specialized tutoring, but those resources weren't available in Darling twenty years ago. That's where this benefit comes in. Thanks to the generosity of all of you, and the people who attended today's events, several charities will be the beneficiaries of much-needed funds."

He looked to Hannah again and felt a wave of love wash over him. She had given him such a great gift, and she didn't even know it. He swallowed around the lump in his throat. "Here's the thing. It's never too late. Never too late to be evaluated or to learn. I'm happy to announce that I'm going to be partnering with two local programs to provide resources and tutoring as early intervention, and also to assist adult non-readers. People like me, who maybe slipped through the cracks and are ready to try again."

A round of applause echoed through the room, and he waited a few moments before he wrapped up.

"Thank you to Hannah Gallagher, the force behind today's events, for all her hard work. I have always been a bit in awe of Hannah's ambition and energy. Now I know it's all fuelled by the biggest heart I've ever known. Thank you, and enjoy the rest of your evening."

More applause echoed as he stepped down from the mic. Oaklee was crying, wiping under her eyes with a finger, and Hannah looked absolutely stunned. He got to his seat, but before retaking it, he leaned over and gave her a small kiss on the lips. He didn't care who knew right now that he'd fallen for her. He'd been waiting a long time to find someone he truly cared about enough to give his heart to. She needed to know he was willing to show the world how he felt about her. He got the feeling not many men had been.

When he finally sat down, he felt about fifty pounds lighter. Now there was just one more thing to do tonight. Tell Hannah the truth about his feelings.

14

Hannah sat through dessert trying to look unaffected while inside her feelings were anything but. She had not expected that, not tonight. Not ever. Cam had explained everything the night of their date by the fire, and she'd accepted it without any qualms. No, she had not expected the grand gesture tonight. Partnering with charities was lovely for him to do, but he had made a personal sacrifice very publicly, and she knew, deep down, that he'd done it for her.

No one had ever done something like that for her before. Not ever. And now it was out there, a big something, and she had no idea what to do with it.

She played with her cheesecake, dipping the tines of the fork into the fluffy confection over and over. He'd looked into her eyes while speaking, and she'd felt something strange and wonderful and terrifying. It had been sneaking up on her for a while. She had gone and fallen in love with Cam.

And love was something she hadn't done for a very long time.

People kept stopping by their table to say hello and to shake Cam's hand. Hannah made sure to smile winningly. After all, she was his date and the coordinator of the event, and it was on her to shine. She laughed and chatted as she always did, as she'd always done no matter the situation. Hannah Gallagher, who always had her shit together. Except right now, something was off. Inside, she was falling apart, and she should be ecstatic. At this moment, she had everything.

The winning auction bids were announced, and the guests began filtering out shortly after nine. Ethan and Willow and Aiden and Laurel disappeared, since their parents were babysitting the kids overnight, and the couples had a rare and treasured night alone. She looked over at Rory, who was positively radiant with his love for Oaklee. It was so beautiful it made her chest hurt. Cam was hugging Oaklee, and he kissed her cheek before she joined Rory to head home. When Cam came back to her side, his eyes were misty.

"Jeez, Collier, you getting all sappy tonight?" She tried a joke to lighten the tightening in her chest. Cam shrugged. "I'm sentimental. Rory's proposing tonight."

Her mouth dropped open. "He is?"

Cam nodded. "I've known it was coming for a while. He came to ask me—and my dad—for permission. It was sweet, actually. I know a lot of Rory's secrets, but I also love him like a brother. I'm happy for them."

"Me, too," Hannah said, but her voice sounded strangled. Cam looked at her strangely.

"You okay, there?"

"I'm fine. Just tired. It was a big day."

"Then let me take you home."

He held her hand and then opened the door for her as she got into the SUV. *I love him.* The words echoed in her head over and over, but she kept trying to push them away. She couldn't love Cam. He had just said he was leaving right after Christmas to go back to Denver. Leaving to go back to his life where he was rich and famous and too…everything for Darling, Vermont.

Too everything for her.

The drive through Darling had a surreal quality. Hannah's insides were in turmoil, but the town was postcard perfect with the recent snow on the ground and the beautiful lights and decorations. It was the Saturday before Christmas. Maybe people inside had gone shopping today and were up wrapping presents. Maybe they were having hot chocolate and watching holiday movies by the light of the tree.

Maybe they were getting engaged. Making love. Holding on for dear life.

Hannah let out a slow breath as Cam pulled up in front of her house. "Can I come in?" he asked softly.

"I'm pretty tired," she answered, avoiding looking in his eyes.

"There's something else going on with you. You haven't looked at me or said a word the whole way home. And I want us to talk about it, Han. We don't have much time left."

That was the problem, wasn't it? Not much time. But a whole Christmas sleigh full of feelings.

"Hannah? Will you look at me?"

She did, her insides quivering. What he'd done tonight was brave and generous and so unexpected. Why had he done it? She was afraid to hear that answer. Afraid and longing to at the same time.

His eyes were dark in the dim light of the vehicle, his lips unsmiling. "I love you, Hannah."

Oh God. He'd said them. The words. The three words she craved and needed and also didn't want to hear from him.

"You don't. It's only been a few weeks."

His eyes were wide and earnest as he held her captive with his gaze. "What does time have to do with anything? I've known you most of my life, if that's the case. But I've never felt this way about anyone before. What I did tonight… I was ready to do it because of you. You have never made me feel stupid or foolish. Instead, you make me feel…like I can do anything."

She could barely breathe. A bit of it was elation, and the remainder was panic. Why was being loved by Cam so frightening? Maybe it wasn't the loving exactly, but what it would mean for them. It was everything tied to it. She shook her head and bit down on her lip.

"You're leaving in a matter of days. We live across the country from each other. This wasn't our agreement."

But his gaze never wavered. When she remained silent, he let out a breath and said, "I didn't want to do this here in my car. But I will if I have to. If that's what it takes. I know it wasn't our agreement, but I want to try to make this work, Han. I've got to go back. We both

know that. But I can fly in, or you could fly to see me…
and in the off-season, we can figure something out. I
know it's not perfect, but don't we owe it to ourselves to
try? This doesn't happen every day." He reached for her
hand. "It's never happened to me. Not like this." He
squeezed her fingers. "Is there even a chance that you
love me too?"

"You don't love me." She met his gaze and thought
back over the last few weeks. "We've had fun, Cam. And
the sex…it's been amazing. But…"

He pulled his hand away and put it on the steering
wheel. "No buts. I was there, Hannah. I was there
when you came apart in my arms and said my name. I
was watching your face every moment. I get that you're
scared. I just don't know why. Why don't you
trust me?"

It wasn't him she didn't trust…not really. She knew
he meant everything he said. But she'd seen the pictures
and TV appearances where sports stars took their glamorous wives and girlfriends. She would never fit in there.
Darling was where she belonged. Big fish, small pond.
What if she gave up everything to be with him, only to
have it crash and burn? She'd have nothing. And how
could she come back home with her tail between her
legs? How could she fail, and so publicly?

And she couldn't say any of this to him, because she
was too afraid. Not just of failure, but of a broken heart.
The last time, she'd bounced back. She wasn't sure she
would after Cam. He was too…everything. Everyone
thought she was so confident. Instead, she was a huge
coward. It was her dirty little secret.

"My life is here," she said quietly. "My business. My family. Everything that is important to me."

Hurt flashed across his face, touching his eyes and making his full lips drop open in surprise.

"So you haven't fallen in love with me, too," he murmured. "Okay then. Okay."

"Cam, I—"

"No, you're right. This wasn't what we agreed to. And I didn't mean to fall for you, Hannah Banana. It complicates everything. But I was willing to give it a try. It doesn't work unless we're both willing to do that."

"You're invited to Christmas Eve at Ethan's," she reminded him. "I don't want you to stay away because of me. And there's New Year's Eve at Rory's…"

"I don't know about Ethan's. I'm going to have to skip New Year's. I'm hoping to be back in the lineup." He looked like he wanted to say more, but reconsidered and sat back in his seat.

Silence fell. Here she was, in a killer dress, all in a plan to finish the evening with him stripping it off her. She'd envisioned getting him out of his suit and into her bed. Now they were just…awkward and sad.

He looked over at her and gave it one last shot. "Hannah, whatever you're afraid of…can't we try to work on it together? I'm afraid, too. The last serious girl-friend I had was crazy about dating a pro athlete and not so happy with the travel schedule and the idea I could change cities and uproot our lives. I have my own hang-ups. It says a lot that I want to try again with you."

She wanted to say yes. But a few weeks together was different than a relationship. Once the newness wore off, would Cam still love the woman she was, deep down? Or would it be like before, where her initiative became ambition, and her organizational abilities became control-freak issues?

When it came right down to it, she didn't trust him enough to believe he'd feel the same after the bloom was off the rose. And she loved him enough to know that to try—and fail—would break her heart irrevocably.

Better to rip the Band-Aid off now, and do it quickly.

"I love that you want to, Cam. I really do. And this has been so amazing. Let's just leave it that way, okay? Our own little Christmas fling that we can look back on with good memories."

"Look back on with good memories?" He shook his head, his voice filled with disbelief. "Sorry, Han. I'll be leaving Darling with a bit of a broken heart. I think I'd rather just forget."

If she was hoping to end this on warm and nostalgic terms, those words disabused her of that idea. She sat back, startled by the coolness in his words. She didn't want this to end with harsh words and regrets, but it looked like it was going to. Because they hadn't had a fling at all. Hearts had been involved, and they both knew it.

She gathered up her clutch purse and put her hand on the door handle. "Good night, Cam. And I'm sorry."

"Me, too," he replied, his voice tight.

※

IT WAS FIVE A.M. ON A SUNDAY MORNING, AND CAM breathed deeply the cold air that had the distinctive ice smell of a hockey rink. Ice time for local teams started at seven, so he'd come out early, needing to feel blades on ice and a stick in his hand. He didn't care that he hadn't been cleared. He was fine. No one else around, no possible contact. He spent the first ten minutes skating, running drills all by himself with only the sound of his skates cutting in the ice for company.

A bucket sat at the edge of the blue line, pucks lined up and waiting. Cam stopped, adjusted the stick in his hands, and made contact with the first one, the weight of the puck and the snap of the stick so familiar that it was like an extension of his own appendages. He made his way down the line, missing the net a few times, correcting and firing puck after puck. Focusing on nothing but the black rubber disks in front of him. When he'd shot the last one, he went to the net, rounded them up, and lined them up again.

Last night, when he'd looked down from the podium, he'd been so sure of her. So certain she shared his feelings. This morning, he was hurt and angry and needing the comfort of the one thing in his life he could count on.

Except in the back of his mind were all the thoughts that had crowded him when he'd first arrived home. What if he sustained another concussion? What if his career ended? Hockey was in his blood and would always be a part of his life in some way. He knew that. But this... He slapped the blade of his stick on the ice, the sound echoing through the arena. How could he be married to this, knowing that even if he stayed healthy, in another ten years he'd be nearing the end of his career?

Maybe the lesson was that nothing was certain. Maybe that's what he'd take back to Denver with him.

The physical exertion felt good, so he kept it up until he looked over and saw Ethan standing at the bench, watching him with a sober expression. Hannah's brother. He wasn't sure he was up to talking to a Gallagher today.

Ethan lifted a hand. "Good morning."

"Hey." Politeness dictated he at least be civil, so he skated over to the boards. "You're here early."

"Eight a.m. ice time with Connor. I was just heading to Mom and Dad's to pick up the boys and I saw your vehicle in the lot. You're feeling better?"

Cam knew Ethan meant the injury, so he nodded. "Yeah. I had one setback when I was home, but I've been symptom free for a bit. Thought I'd lace up this morning before the ice gets busy. Feels good."

"You don't look like it feels good. You look like you're ready to clock someone." Ethan grinned and took a step backward, out of reach.

"Hannah dumped me last night." Cam hadn't expected to say the words, but they came out of his mouth anyway. He gripped the stick tighter. "I didn't see it coming."

Ethan's face flattened in surprise. "She dumped you? What the hell?"

"Just what I asked myself. I didn't sleep much, but this morning, I thought this might help clear my head."

"And has it?"

"Not really. I read her all wrong, Ethan. Anyway, maybe it's good you know. I don't want things to be weird with the family. I promised Connor I'd practice with him, and I will in the next day or two. But I'm gonna skip Christmas Eve, and I'm heading back to Denver right after the holiday."

Ethan's eyes held disappointment. "I'm sorry, Cam. We have all been rooting for the two of you. Hannah is great and deserves to be happy. She also needs to be jolted out of her comfort zone."

"I don't know what to say to that one."

Ethan laughed. "Believe me, I do not want the gory details. But she lit up every time you were together. You did, too. Darling and her business here and the big family…it's low risk for her. She never has to fail here. You represent something crazy, and you don't come with guarantees. Even if she does care for you like you do for her, that would probably stop her up."

Cam leaned against the boards. He hadn't thought about that before. Was Hannah just really afraid to take a chance? Did she maybe love him too?

"How do you know all this?" he asked Ethan.

Ethan smiled. "Bro. I've known Hannah all of her life. We're the oldest two. To be honest, I think we both felt the weight of expectations. By the time we were in school, there were six of us. Mom and Dad were always busy. Hannah and I had to step up a lot, and she got used to meeting expectations. I think she's always been worried about what would happen if she didn't."

"You didn't feel that way?"

"Hannah was the only girl until the twins came along. I had my brothers to distract me. And I still felt that sometimes. Until my wife died. Then I let go of expectations… Well, I didn't at first. But I did once I fell in love with Willow."

His face softened as he said his wife's name. It was sweet and sent a bittersweet jolt to Cam's heart. Did he look like that when he spoke about Hannah?

Lord, he was a lovesick puppy, wasn't he?

Ethan gave him a nod. "Maybe you shouldn't give up yet. Hannah's stubborn, but if anyone can change her mind, it's you."

But Cam had his own issues. He didn't want to have to beg and convince someone to be with him. He'd done that before with Alyssa, and it had flopped. No, Hannah needed to be all in, meet-in-the-middle, ready to try if this was going to work.

"Listen, thanks for the advice. I appreciate it. Not sure it'll change anything, but it helped my state of mind."

"No problem. Hey, none of us would mind having you officially be part of the family. And now I should go. I gotta get the boys and make sure we're back."

Ethan waved goodbye, and Cam set to work cleaning up his pucks, changing out of his skates, and stowing his stuff in his SUV.

Then he went home for a shower and breakfast. And a long day ahead of him that didn't include Hannah.

It was a bitter pill to swallow.

15

Hannah wiped her face with another tissue and cursed out loud as she dropped it in the wastebasket. She didn't cry over guys. She just didn't. She hadn't since Liam had said so many things that had cut her to the quick the day he'd broken up with her.

Back then, she'd cried because Liam had turned all the things she liked about herself into faults. Now, she was crying because Cam loved her for those things, and she couldn't bring herself to trust him. To trust that it would last. Or worse, he loved Darling Hannah. But would he love Denver Hannah? Would his friends like her, or would they wonder what in the world he was thinking?

She kicked the garbage can, spilling soiled tissues over the bathroom floor. For a confident, strong woman, she had huge self-esteem problems.

Her dirty little secret.

She'd sent Cam away and was now sitting alone in

her little house in her little town, only a few days away from Christmas and hating every moment.

A cup of coffee restored her a little, along with a bowl of berries she picked at while sitting at her kitchen table. She didn't want to stay here alone and didn't want to go anywhere, either. Not looking like this. Her eyes were red and swollen, and her hair was a rat's nest pushed up in a messy bun and held with an elastic. She dressed in yoga pants and a sweatshirt of Cam's that was much too big for her. It still smelled like him, and she wrapped her arms around herself to intensify the scent. She was going to miss him so much. His smile and laugh, his stupidly thick eyelashes…everything.

Her cell rang, and she saw Rory's number. A lump formed in her throat. Did he already know about the breakup and was calling to read her the riot act? It was no secret everyone loved Cam. He could do no wrong. Even her own family would take his side. Not that there were sides to take. It was just… Oh, why had she thought a fling would be a good idea?

The ringing stopped, but a few moments later, it started again. Worry settled in the pit of her stomach. What if something was wrong with their folks or one of the kids? She took a breath and answered.

"Hey, Han," Rory said in reply. He sounded far too cheerful for there to be anything wrong.

"What's up? It's barely nine on a Sunday morning."

"Oh, you know. Just having coffee. Making some eggs. Picking a date for a wedding."

The line went silent as what he'd just said sank in, and then tears burned her eyes again. "Oh, Rory. You proposed last night?" She'd forgotten Cam had mentioned it, she was so wrapped up in her own broken heart.

"I did. And she said yes."

"Well, of course she did." Hannah didn't have to force happiness into her voice. Oaklee and Rory were so clearly made for each other. "Congratulations, little brother."

"Yeah, well, you're next," he said joyfully. Hannah's chest tightened as she fought to keep her voice light.

"Oh, there's no rush there. Have you told Mom and Dad?"

"Yeah, we told them just now. But you're the first of the sibs. You're my big sis, you know? And Oaklee loves you."

Aw, heck, now she was definitely misty. "I love her, too. I'm thrilled for you both."

"Good, because we're already talking about having Cam as best man and you standing up with Oaklee. Awesome, right?"

It was such a blow to her already tender feelings that she felt sick to her stomach. "Aw, there's lots of time to plan. You need to celebrate now." She wasn't going to ruin his perfect day with her drama.

"All right. Love you, Han."

She could finish the call without sobbing. She could.

"Love you, too, Rory."

She ended the call, but then the sobs came. Big, gulping, gasping ones that made her head ache. She wasn't sure if she was more hurt that she and Cam had broken up, or upset at herself for ruining everything because she was a coward.

Her hand hovered near her phone. She could call him, tell him she'd been wrong. But it wouldn't take away her fears or make everything okay. So she withdrew her hand and laid her head on the table. After a while, the weeping ceased, and she got up and drank a glass of water and took something for the headache. Then she got under the blanket on the sofa and stared at the Christmas tree they'd decorated together until her lids grew heavy and she fell asleep.

Monday she was back at her desk, clearing away backlogged items on her to-do list now that the literacy benefit was over. Oaklee was handling the final tallies, and in the new year, they'd look at dispersing the funds to the selected charities. It had taken a lot of Hannah's work hours, so she was happy to throw herself back into her job.

And if she used work as a distraction, so what? She hadn't heard a peep from Cam. Christmas Eve was right around the corner. She would go on as usual. Efficient, energetic, driven Hannah Gallagher, who was a whiz at biz but sucked at relationships.

Every time her phone rang, she wondered if it was him. Or if it would be one of her family asking her what the heck was wrong with her brain. But nothing. Either Cam had kept quiet, or they were all buzzing around talking about it behind her back. She wasn't really sure which she preferred. Generally, she was a deal-with-it-straight-on kind of woman. But now…

She missed him. The reason why she kept staring at the phone or out her office window was because she wanted to hear his voice. Get a glimpse of him.

The day ended, she packed up her tote bag, and walked home in the dark. Her house was dark, too, and she flicked on lights to take away some of the emptiness. Maybe she was like Oaklee and needed a dog. Or a couple of cats. She could become a crazy cat lady.

Dinner was something easy to throw together: roasted squash, with marinara and goat cheese. She supposed she could wrap presents, turn on the TV and watch one of the zillion holiday specials that were on. She still had the present she'd bought for Cam sitting in her closet. She'd had a jersey from the Darling peewee team—where he'd first started playing—made up with his name and number. It was custom, so she couldn't take it back. And he still hadn't called or texted, so giving it to him was out of the question. He clearly wanted nothing to do with her.

The doorbell rang and she jumped, the blanket she'd put over her legs as she drank her after-dinner tea sliding off her lap. She wanted it to be him, though she had no idea what to say if it really was him on her front step.

She opened the door and instead found Laurel staring back at her. Her sister-in-law, and one of her dearest friends. Laurel held up a bottle of wine. "I figured you might need this after the last few days."

Hannah's lip wobbled. "So you heard?"

"Yeah, I heard. Cam told Ethan yesterday morning. Ethan told the rest of us. When no one heard from you all day today, I figured I'd better check on you."

"I'm fine."

"Oh, girlfriend." Laurel stepped inside and handed over the wine. "You are so not fine."

"Well, I will be." Hannah lifted her chin, trying to stay strong while she was incredibly touched that Laurel was being a true friend.

Laurel hung up her coat, took the wine from Hannah's hands again, and shook her head. "It's cute that you think that. Come on, Han. It's Cam freaking Collier we're talking about here. Hot, rich, nice guy, and he loves you. How can you possibly be fine?"

The doorbell rang again, and Hannah's heart leapt. She opened it to find Willow standing there, holding another bottle of wine and a paper bag in her opposite fist.

"What is this, an intervention?"

Willow grinned. "If it needs to be. It's cold as balls out here. Let me in."

Hannah stepped aside. She wasn't going to win this one, and she knew it. And she probably deserved it. She'd done her fair share of nosing in when Laurel and Willow had been dating her brothers.

Laurel took over opening the wine, and Willow took a container of homemade truffles out of the paper bag. "Dark chocolate. Excellent for pairing with that red. And by the look of your eyes, wine and chocolate are very, very necessary. What the hell are you doing, walking away from a man like that?"

Laurel handed Hannah a glass and looked over at Willow. "Hey. We're not here to judge. Hannah has her reasons."

"Just like you had yours," Hannah said to Willow, gesturing with the glass in her hand. "Don't forget, you walked away from Ethan, too."

"Because I was stupid. We're here to keep you from making the same mistake."

Hannah laughed. "I love you guys."

"We love you, too. Let's go sit down, and you can spill your guts. Then we'll figure out what's next."

Hannah's heart warmed. Even though she'd been afraid to see anyone, having her two closest friends come to the rescue made the crushing pain in her chest ease just a bit. They went into the living room, where Hannah's tree was lit and casting a gorgeous glow over the room.

"Oh, now, that's a dandy," Laurel said. "George pick that out for you?"

"George and…and Cam."

Willow sank down into a chair and took a sip of wine. "Okay, babes. What happened? Because two nights ago, he was looking at you like you hung the moon and stars. And you were making googly eyes at him, too."

Hannah sipped the wine—it was very good, and she savoured the taste on her tongue for a moment. "I got cold feet, you guys. That's it in a nutshell. I'm terrified. So it was just better to end it now, before things got out of hand."

Laurel burst out laughing and reached for a truffle.

"Out of hand? Sweet pea, it's been out of hand since the first night he stayed over. Lordy, you two can't be in the same room without giving off sparks. That kind of thing can be scary. Really intense, really fast."

Willow nodded. "It was that way with Ethan. Scared me to death."

"If you guys are going to talk about having sex with my brothers, I'm going to need more wine and a set of earplugs." But Hannah grinned, her heart a little lighter.

"Then let's talk about you and Cam. What's got you so scared?"

Hannah took a long drink. Then another. The answer was simple yet so difficult to say. "Honestly? Change. I'm afraid of all the changes it would mean to my life, and I'm really not sure I'd fit into his life at all. He doesn't have a...a normal life like the rest of us."

"So you're just going to give up without giving it a shot? How do you know you won't fit in if you don't try? I have a hard time believing that Cam is any different back in Colorado than he is here. He's a good guy with a good heart. He works hard. He isn't a jerk or a snob. He never behaves in a way that gets him in the news, either. It's not like he'd go back there and pull a Mr. Hyde."

Hannah tried a truffle, focusing on the dark, rich flavours. She brushed her fingers on her jeans and let out a long sigh. "Look, you guys. I know it's me. But I guess it's just...this is Christmas, and Darling, and maybe we got caught up in something that won't last. How can I uproot my life for that?"

Willow's gaze widened. "Did he ask you that? To move to Denver?"

"No, he just said he wanted to talk and work something out. Not say goodbye. He told me he…" She swallowed around the lump that had come and gone a million times since Saturday night. "He told me he loved me."

Laurel and Willow practically swooned before her eyes. "And you said no?"

"What if it all goes wrong? What if I get my heart broken?"

Her question hung in the air for a few moments. Then Laurel came and sat beside her and took her hand. "People survive broken hearts all the time. Sometimes we have a life all planned out for ourselves and something throws a monkey wrench into it. But it doesn't mean we stop trying."

"But what if I've built a life I love?"

Willow studied her glass and then looked up, her eyes soft with understanding. "Hey, I get it. Ethan stepped into my life and disrupted all the peace and tranquility I'd built for myself. I had made my world a safe space, and he forced me out of it into something risky and unpredictable. And I'm not sorry, of course I'm not. But I understand the fear, Hannah. I do."

Hannah reached over and took Willow's hand. "I know you do."

Laurel nodded. "And after my divorce, I was really not looking for a romance. Particularly not with Aiden. But there he was. I'd had my perfect life and lost it. I wasn't so into giving someone that much influence again."

"But it changed for you both. It doesn't mean it would for me."

"Ah," Willow said wisely. "That's where I think you're wrong. The truth of the matter is, our lives would look very different if we hadn't ended up being loved by —and loving—two fine men. It wouldn't be like this for me with anyone else. How about you, Laurel?"

Laurel shook her head. "Aiden's it. He tells me the truth when it's hard, and he loves me all the time. No one else gets me like him. And I can totally be myself and know that it's okay."

Willow looked at Hannah. "Ever felt that way about anyone, Han?"

They were so right. Why would this be the same as before if everything else was different? She was different. Cam was, too. He understood her when others didn't. Got her insecurities and loved her because of them. "I've never loved anyone like this before. It scares me to death."

"That's how you know it's real," Laurel announced, and reached for the other wine bottle. When she'd topped up the glasses, she held hers out for a toast. "To love. It's crazy and scary and wonderful. And totally worth it."

Willow held out her glass, a smile playing on her lips. Finally, Hannah held out hers, too, and closed her eyes and she touched her rim to theirs. "To love. God help me."

They finished off the bottle, and by the time they got

to the end, they'd come up with a pseudo plan that Hannah would re-evaluate when they were all sober. But before the two women put on their coats to leave, they made Hannah promise to go through with the plan.

Rory—the only Gallagher man who wasn't on diaper duty—came and picked them up and drove them home, and Hannah ate the last truffle before heading to bed. She had a big day tomorrow, and only a short window of time to get what she needed.

16

The last thing Cam wanted to do today was go to the park and pose for family pictures on the Kissing Bridge. Oaklee was adamant, though, because he was so rarely home, and they were hardly ever all together. He could think of other ways to spend Christmas Eve. Watching movies and having a few beers with his dad. Doing some light conditioning, a skate at the rink maybe. Definitely not something in public. And hopefully not with Hannah there. She had broken it off, and she hadn't texted him or called, not once. He was more than hurt by it. He missed her. It said a lot that she could walk away so easily.

"Cam, come on! The photographer is going to be there right at two."

"Fine." He rolled his eyes and left his old room behind. He wasn't sure when he'd be home again after this trip. For Oaklee and Rory's wedding, certainly. But an extended visit… It would probably be a long time. To his surprise, he felt a bit homesick already about it.

Oaklee went in her car, while he went with their parents. Oaklee would be leaving afterward to go to Ethan's for Christmas Eve with the Gallaghers. His folks were going out to a neighbours', as they did every year. He'd be sitting home alone.

After they got parked, they walked the short distance to the bridge. Oaklee was already there with Rory, and the photographer appeared to be making some adjustments before starting the shoot. Cam stood back and enjoyed a bittersweet moment. His sister and best friend looked so happy together. Oaklee was radiant, and Rory couldn't stop smiling. Rory had brought their dog along, too. The caramel-coloured ball of fluff pranced around their feet until Rory gave a command and offered a treat. They were already a family, weren't they? He had a vision of his sister as a mom and got so sentimental he had to turn away. He'd be an uncle someday.

But it was bittersweet, because he didn't want to be standing here alone. God, he'd come home, and all he'd wanted was peace and quiet and to get back to Denver as soon as possible. He still wanted that, but he wanted so much more. He wanted Hannah, and her love, and the privilege of loving her in return. Funny how the first victory felt hollow without the second.

The dog was behaving so nicely that they decided to snap the engagement pics first. Rory and Oaklee had made their relationship official on the bridge in a very public fashion; it only seemed fitting that their pictures be there as well. Oaklee's hair was down, and she wore a red coat and scarf, looking festive and bright as Rory put his arms around her. The pup sat at their feet. Then there were shots with them kneeling by the dog, and a kiss with the leash dropped by their feet. Cam would have thought it hokey if it weren't so genuinely sweet and celebratory.

Then it was time for the family. Oaklee, Cam, and their parents posed at the arc of the bridge, and once again, Cam's latent sentimental streak made an appearance. His family was pretty amazing when all was said and done, and he appreciated them more than they could know.

He was going to miss them when he returned to the team.

"Cam, we'd like for you to change your shirt," Oaklee said, putting her hand on his arm.

"What?" His mood took a shift into annoyed. "What's wrong with my sweater?"

"It's missing something."

That was not Oaklee's voice. It was Hannah's, and it made his heart stop. He turned around to find her standing there, holding out a box, but what was more, she was wearing his team jersey.

She looked adorable. He couldn't stop staring at her, as if afraid she would go away if he so much as blinked. "Han," he said softly, and she smiled a little.

"It's your Christmas gift."

"You want me to open it here?"

She nodded. "Yes, please." She held out the box with hands clad in thin gloves the same shade of blue as was in the jersey. He didn't understand why she was wearing it, but one thing at a time.

Everyone had moved off, giving them a smidge of

privacy. He took the box and placed it on the end of the concrete wall of the bridge, then undid the wide bow and ribbon holding it together. When he lifted the lid, a smile lit his face.

"My peewee jersey!"

"Only a few sizes larger. So you can wear it now."

"Right now?"

"It's big enough to fit over gear. I think it'll fit over your sweater."

He lifted it up. It was a home game jersey, white with red and black, with his name and number on it. The same number he'd had since he was eight.

"This is cool." He pulled it over his head and down over his sweater. It felt a little awkward, but he didn't care. "I love it, Hannah. But why here? Why now?" He looked her in the eyes. "After what happened, why give me a present at all?"

She came forward and took his hands. "Because I was afraid, and I let that colour my decision. I lied to you, Cam, and that was the worst mistake of my life. I hope it's not too late. You should know that I love you, too. I fought it the whole time, but at the benefit, when you got up to speak…I realized exactly the kind of man you are, and I couldn't fight it anymore. Then when you said you loved me…" She stopped, bit down on her lip.

"You bolted," he finished for her.

She nodded.

"Why are you wearing my jersey?" he asked. He wanted to hope but wasn't sure he should. He needed her to say the words, but more than that, he needed her to mean them.

"Because I don't want to be afraid to take chances and miss out on something incredible. I've spent my whole life being the responsible one, the one who always lives up to expectations, the one people can rely on. And that worked for me. It validated me when people said I was bossy or too loud or too smart. Sliding into that role gave me a measure of safety, so I wouldn't have to risk being somewhere else and having those attributes... thrown in my face."

He was starting to put the pieces together. "You mentioned your ex before, but it's more than that, isn't it? It's me?"

"Not you. No one has ever accepted me as you have. But more... What happens if I go to Denver with you? Meet your teammates and their wives and girlfriends, the puck bunnies outside the dressing room? What are they going to think of me? I'm an achiever, Cam, and I can organize things. I don't know how to be...your girlfriend."

He wanted to say, "Is that all?", but he knew that this was so important to her it had nearly driven them apart.

"Hannah. The only thing you have to do to be my girlfriend is love me. Everything else we'll figure out. And some of those people might surprise you. We all have our hang-ups." He lifted his hand and touched her cheek. "I wanted to come to you and beg you to reconsider. But I was so afraid you'd decide it wasn't worth it—I wasn't worth it—and walk away anyway. We can figure it out. All I need from you is a promise that you'll be there with me."

She nodded, her eyes shining. "I want to. I love you, Cam. It took me by surprise and blew me away, but I fell for you hard. I'm not ready to say goodbye to Darling, but I'm more than willing to travel back and forth for a little bit and then make bigger plans."

"I was thinking I could come back and do a hockey school in the off-season. Spend some more time in Darling with my family. And yours."

"And I could maybe split time between Denver and here."

"See? We're doing it already."

She looked up at him and smiled, her eyes shining. "I'm sorry. I'm sorry for what I said after the benefit, and sorry we wasted time. I was foolish and afraid. For all my business smarts, I am not a risk taker in my personal life. But I know better than anyone that the higher risks yield the best returns."

"Mmm. I love it when you talk like that."

She burst out laughing. Then she lifted her chin and said, "Now will you kiss me please? I'm dying over here, wanting one. Wanting you."

He didn't need any prodding. He stepped the few inches closer and pulled her into his arms, claiming her winter-kissed lips. Suddenly, everything in the world was right again. She gripped the fabric of his jersey and pulled him closer until they heard whistles and clapping from the end of the bridge.

"Oh, geez," she said, putting her forehead against his chest.

"Might as well get used to it," he said. "You kissed

me on the Kissing Bridge, and you know what that means."

"That our love is gonna last forever? You don't really believe in that stuff, do you?"

He cupped her face in his hands. "Look at your family and tell me it doesn't work." He grinned. "Now. We have Christmas Eve at Ethan's to get through. We're going to eat food and play with kids and you're gonna hold babies, and then, after they've had a goodnight story from their Uncle Cam, I'm going to take you home and make this one Christmas to remember. You still have that gold dress, right?"

Her cheeks were pink with cold, but her blush deepened as she nodded. "I might have."

"Good. And when it fits your schedule, I'm going to fly you to Denver so you can see my apartment and meet my houseplants and some of the guys that are my other family."

"I love you, Cam."

"I love you, too, Hannah Banana. I'm glad you changed your mind."

She laughed and took his hand. "You're lucky. Because once I set my mind to something…"

He squeezed back and wondered if he'd ever thought he could be this happy. "You get the job done. I know." He planted a kiss on her temple. "In fact, I'm counting on it."

FEBRUARY

Claire Gallagher sat with the rest of her family on a Saturday night, watching the hockey game. Cam was playing, and everyone was gathered in John and Moira's living room, having a few drinks, eating popcorn, and cursing out the ref. Everyone except Hannah. She was in Denver for a few weeks, and things were hot and heavy with her and Cam. Claire looked around and found her twin, Cait, looking at her phone. Something had been off with her lately, though Claire couldn't put her finger on what.

"Look, you guys! Hannah's on TV!"

There was a break as the goal net had come off the post, and the camera panned around and settled on Hannah. Hannah was dressed in a team jersey and had her hair up. She looked…happy. And beautiful. But it did mean that Claire and Cait were the only ones left who were single. Rory and Oaklee had a wedding date for the summer, and it wouldn't surprise her if either Willow or Laurel got pregnant again.

The camera moved away after a few moments, and the game recommenced. Aiden went to get another beer and put his hand on her shoulder. "You okay, squirt?"

"I'm fine. Hannah looks good."

"Well, she decided to stop letting fear drive her decisions. And now she's happy, so good for her."

Claire felt Cait's gaze on the two of them. "Do you think they'll get married?"

"Yeah. Hannah's gonna want some babies soon, and since they can't keep their hands off each other…"

"Aiden!" Moira's voice came across the living room. "Eeew."

"Sorry, Ma." But he grinned and winked at Claire. "You want another?"

"Naw, I'm good. I'm going to go to bed soon anyway."

But before she did, she looked around the room, her heart filled with love for her family and a little bit of longing at being left out. Her gaze touched Cait's, and they shared a thought, as they often did as twins. *Sucks not having a partner.*

But Claire hadn't given up hope. And she wanted a happy ending for her sister, too.

Everyone deserved their own happy ever after.

ABOUT THE AUTHOR

While bestselling author Donna Alward was busy studying Austen, Eliot and Shakespeare, she was also losing herself in the breathtaking stories created by romance novelists like LaVyrle Spencer and Judith McNaught. Several years after completing her degree she decided to write a romance of her own and it was true love! Five years and ten manuscripts later she sold her first book and launched a new career. While her heartwarming stories of love, hope, and homecoming have been translated into several languages, hit bestseller lists and won awards, her very favorite thing is when she hears from happy readers.

Donna lives on Canada's east coast. When she's not writing she enjoys reading (of course!), knitting, gardening, cooking…and is a Masterpiece addict. You can visit her on the web at www.DonnaAlward.com and join her mailing list at www.DonnaAlward.com/newsletter .

Find your next great Donna Alward read at
http://www.donnaalward.com/bookshelf